OTHER BOOKS BY ASHLEY FONTAINNE

The Magnolia Series (written with Lillian Hansen):
Blood Ties
Blood Loss
Blood Stain

Mystery/suspense novels:
Fatal Agreements
Suicide Lake
Empty Shell
Night Court
Whispered Pain
Number Seventy-Five

Eviscerating the Snake Trilogy:
Accountable to None
Zero Balance
Adjusting Journal Entries

Paranormal/suspense:
Growl
The Lie
Operation Jade Helmet

Poetry and Short Stories:
Ruined Wings
Fine as Frog Hair
Ramblings of a Mad Southern Woman

OTHER BOOKS BY ASHLEY FONTAINNE

TAINTED
FUTURE

AS THE DEAD RISE THE LIVING SEARCH
FOR SHELTER

ASHLEY FONTAINNE

Cover and Interior book design by One of a Kind Covers

TAINTED FUTURE
Copyright © by Ashley Fontainne 2016, 2017, 2018

Published by RMSW Press, LLC
ISBN 13: 978-0692681923
ISBN 10: 0692681922

TABLE OF CONTENTS

Chapter 1 - Waking up in Hell

Monday, December 22nd – 5:15 a.m. – Mountain Standard Time

COOPER HOLLINGSWORTH stares at the bloody snow. The crimson patches make the thick, white powder look like someone tossed buckets of red juice all over the ground, creating the ghastly illusion he is surrounded by slushies made from human blood. Mind reeling, he barely notices the lone streetlight flickering, bouncing flashes of light across the area. To him, it feels like watching a horror movie and at any second, eerie music will fill the gas station's parking lot.

He wishes a director would yell "cut" and the nightmare would be over.

That isn't going to happen.

The knowledge this is all real makes him puke. Bending over, he vomits until nothing remains to expel from his body except saliva.

The gun in his hand feels like it weighs thirty pounds, but he won't put it back inside the holster. It is too risky. More of them may be lurking about, drawn to the sound of the shots he fired only minutes ago.

Eight spent shell casings rest in small divots in the snow next to his feet. The wind picks up speed, stirring the top layer of fresh powder into a whirling vortex of white. Cold shards pepper his exposed face, making his eyes water, but the wind isn't the only reason tears streak down his cheeks and chin.

"This isn't real. It can't be." He whispers to the dead corpses on the ground. "God, Karla. I'm so sorry."

Fear reaches inside his chest and latches its cold, strong tentacles around his heart. Pausing to listen for signs of any others, his fingers twitch with nervous anticipation. Hearing nothing, he blows out a huff of air, watching the vapors linger above him before disappearing into the darkness.

The earlier, continual sounds of explosions, gunfire, and people screaming had faded into sporadic bouts of noise after leaving Steamboat Springs. For hours, he and Karla wound their way through the treacherous, twisty roads leading out of Steamboat toward Denver. Karla had been in a state of shock, alternating between crying and yelling while he dodged stalled vehicles and mangled corpses.

The carnage surrounding him fades out. Disturbing memories of how they ended up on the run for their lives fill his vision. He leans against the cold hood of the SUV and weeps.

***

"Cooper? Honey, wake up. Something's wrong."

Every muscle in his body aches from a long afternoon the day before hiking through the snow-covered trails. Even though Karla had a map, they still managed to get turned around and ended up wandering for hours. By the time they arrived back at their vehicle, both were cold and exhausted.

Groaning, he rolls over and snuggles closer to his wife's warm body. He opens one eye and scans the dark room, guessing it is close to dawn.

"Go back to sleep, baby. We're in the mountains. It's probably a moose or deer foraging around outside. Maybe even a cougar out hunting for breakfast."

Karla's grip intensifies on his arm; slender fingers dig into the flesh. "I know what animals sound like, Cooper Hollingsworth. They don't scream like humans!"

The terror in his wife's voice forces him to open both eyes. Pulling Karla closer, assuming she is freaked out from a nightmare, he tries to offer comfort, but his doubts about what she heard vanish the second several shrill, ear-piercing screams fill the dark bedroom. The wails send chills up his spine. He recognizes the abject fear in the voices.

Fully awake, he reverts to cop mode, motioning for Karla to remain quiet while he eases out from under the covers. Padding across the cold hardwood, he reaches the bookcase where his cell and gun sit. Snatching up his pistol, he peers out the window while simultaneously dialing 9-1-1.

"We're sorry, all circuits are busy. Please try your call again later."

He hears the words in his ear from the robotic voice, yet they really don't register because his attention is on three women running through the parking lot. The new layer of snow and ice on the pavement makes their attempts to flee a wasted effort. They slip and slide across the ground. One of them falls, and the remaining two scramble to pick her up.

The parking lot lights of the rental condos provide enough light for him to see every detail. He recognizes the girls from their long, bright red hair—the triplets named Margo, Margie, and Marie. They'd bumped into each other while unpacking their vehicles the day before.

The three young women were celebrating their twenty-first birthdays in the awe-inspiring mountains of Steamboat Springs. The girls are beautiful, full of energy and spunk, and only a few inches shy of his 6'1" frame. Even though he is celebrating his anniversary with his lovely bride, he couldn't help but admire their curves and sexy smiles while they carted overstuffed suitcases from their vehicle.

Margo mentioned in passing their boyfriends surprised them with the combined Christmas and birthday present of a week in the mountains. Margie had laughed and said the surprise was really on their men because they'd missed their flight from Boise and would have to drive in. Marie giggled while holding a box full of liquor, commenting about how the boys would miss out on ravishing their drunk girlfriends the first night.

Are the men chasing the girls their boyfriends or just locals who decided to take advantage of three women alone?

Stepping away from the window, he looks around for his clothes.

"What's going on, honey? Did you see anyone?" Karla whispers while turning on the bedside lamp.

"Looks like a major falling out between the triplets and their dates. Stay here and keep trying to call 9-1-1." He yanks on a pair of jeans and a coat before sliding on his slippers. "I'm going to help those girls. Seems like the boyfriends—"

"No! Oh, my God! Margo! Margie! Somebody help us!"

Double-checking the magazine to make sure it is full; he glances over at Karla. Her big, green eyes are the size of saucers.

Darting out of the bed, she makes a beeline for her cell phone. "Quit talking and get! I'm on it."

"Give them code 10-17 and advise out-of-state law enforcement is on scene and armed. I don't want them shooting me."

Karla nods while putting her robe on. Turning, he races down the stairs, opens the front door, and is immediately slapped in the face by the cold mountain air. How the girls are outside without coats on—and the men only in their underwear—he cannot fathom. Based on the impact to his skin, the temperature hovers near zero.

Forcing himself to take even, calculated steps on the treacherous walkway, he makes it out to the parking lot.

The first orange and yellow rays of the sun peek over Mount Werner, but have yet to touch the valley, forcing him to rely on instincts while navigating in the dark. In the distance, the faint sound of yelling and the distinct *pop pop pop* of gunfire make his skin prickle.

What the Hell is going on?

The screaming stops and he knows this isn't a good sign. His heart pounds in his ears, adrenaline in overdrive as he rounds the corner of the building, rather surprised none of the other vacationers are outside trying to help. He brushes the thought away, remembering he isn't in a small, southern town in Arkansas. This is Colorado, and though Steamboat isn't a huge town, it is bigger than Malvern. Obviously, the big city mentality of "mind your own business" reigns supreme.

The bright lights cast from several security lamps in the parking lot guide the way and allow him a full visual of what is happening to Marie, Margo, and Margie. All three girls are down, their fire-engine red hair in stark contrast against the white snow. Two of the men appear to be fighting with each other over one, and the remaining male has his head down on...

"No way!"

His brain tries to comprehend the improbable scene. Raising the pistol, he stops about twenty yards away and plants his feet.

"Police! Hands up and get away from them right now or I'll shoot. This is your only warning."

The man closest to him, the one with his face buried in the stomach of one of the triplets, raises his head and turns toward the sound of Cooper's voice. A sick feeling spreads throughout his chest. The movement is nothing near the fluid motions of a person and reminds him of several horror movies he'd watched with his kids—the kind filmed in a jumbled mash of shots where the monster lurches and shudders with unnatural, inhuman steps.

Acid burns in his stomach when he realizes the man's face is covered in blood. The wind shifts and the rank stench of bowels make him gag. Entrails hang from the man's mouth; tendrils of steam from warm flesh surround his head. The man continues chewing while his hand shovels more intestines into an already full mouth.

The girl is dead. No one could remain quiet while being eviscerated or survive with an empty body cavity.

Without hesitating, he fires. The bullet tears through the man's chest, center mass, yet doesn't faze him in the least. The impact knocks him to the ground, but before Cooper can blink twice, the man is on his feet, making short order of the distance between them.

Motion to the right catches his attention. The other two men stopped fighting, drawn to the sound of the gunshot. Stunned and in shock the bullet hadn't killed the first man, he shuts out the crazy thoughts spinning through his mind. He pushes away the law-abiding cop, the one trained to diffuse a volatile situation with minimal force; brushes off what the aftermath might be when the incident makes the news. It will be the kind filled with headlines about a rogue cop losing control and blowing holes in innocent civilians.

He doesn't care because something is very, very wrong with these men. Alarm bells ring inside his mind, warning him if he doesn't take out the three bastards, they'll continue killing until someone else intervenes.

While exhaling, he steadies his aim and fires again. The round pierces the space between the man's eyes, blowing chunks of brain matter, skull, and gore as it exits the back. The body collapses in midstride with a loud *thump*.

Turning his focus on the other two, who are less than ten feet away, he doesn't hesitate. In less than two seconds, he takes in every visual, auditory, and sensory input. The boys—*no, things*—are directly under the light in the parking lot. There is a weird, bluish array of zigzagging lines all over their bodies. The coppery odor of blood fills the air.

A shudder of fear wracks his body. There are no puffs of air streaming from their mouths; no rise and fall of their chests.

They aren't breathing.

Both sets of hands are covered in red. Blood dribbles down their chins and onto bare chests. One opens his mouth and hisses, almost like a pissed off cat. Each has the same awkward gait as the other. Their eyes are solid black.

Acid? PCP? Something new? What kind of drug turns eyes black as coal and stops a person from breathing, yet allows them to keep moving? Even the sclera is dark! Like that matters, dumbass. They. Aren't. Breathing.

"One more step and I'll—"

The grumbling, guttural roar from both men makes sweat burst from Cooper's skin. Two quick, well-placed shots later, their halting advancement is over. All three men are down, dark rivulets of thick, mahogany-colored blood seeps from their wounds into the snow. A light groan from one of the girls causes his heart to skip two beats.

Sidestepping the three dead men, he checks on the girl. The other two are dead, ripped to pieces as though a horde of wild hogs tore them apart. He swallows the burning stomach juices rumbling inside him.

He cannot tell which sister he is looking at because the girl's face is gone. How she is still alive—at least enough to moan—is beyond his comprehension.

Crouching next to her shredded and mangled body, he knows she won't last another two minutes. The amount of blood loss is staggering, and even if she was at a hospital and on an operating table, she stands no shot of surviving. Bubbles of blood ooze from the gaping wound in her neck. He can see every one of her white teeth—including the back molars—since the skin and most of the flesh on her face has been torn off. Rather than let her die in the cold snow alone, he reaches out, takes her frozen hand in his, and squeezes and whispers, "Go in peace. I got them. Go in peace."

Tears cloud his vision, thinking how close in age the girl is to his own kids. He would want someone to offer a warm hand and kind words to one of his children if ever—God forbid—they were in a similar situation.

A memory of the last words his mother said to his father in the hospital pops into his mind, and they seem appropriate. "Let the angels come and take you away to a place where you'll never hurt again."

"What the hell did you do?"

He jerks at the sound of a man's voice behind him, raising his gun. He lets out a small sigh when realizing the kid—no older than eighteen—poses no threat. Other than holding a cell phone in front of him, the boy is unarmed.

"That's your contribution to this? Standing there filming? Why don't you call for help instead of trying to be the next YouTube star?"

"Screw you, old man. I'm not the one who just shot and killed three people in cold blood."

Shaking his head, Cooper turns his attention back to the girl. Her entire body quakes and then tenses up. With one last burst of air, she is gone. He recites the Lord's Prayer in silence before rising and glancing over at the kid with a wild mop of curly, black hair. He's turned the camera on the corpses of the men. Irritated and ashamed at how the upcoming generation seem more obsessed with making a name for themselves rather than helping a fellow human being in distress, he comes up behind the boy and snatches the phone.

"Hey! That's mine!"

"Never said it wasn't. Keep your pants on, junior. I just need to call for help."

"Won't do you any good. Phones are out. Net is too. Power probably won't be on much longer, either. Haven't you been watching the news, old man?"

He ignores the brash upstart, clicks over to the keypad, and dials 9-1-1. Just like earlier, he is greeted with the same message.

"Shit!" He hands the phone back to the kid. "Where's the nearest police station?"

"Like I know! I'm not from around here. I tried calling the cops before I went outside. I've been calling them for hours. Nothing happens; no one answers, just some weird recording. I heard gunshots, so figured I'd at least get evidence of what was going on to give the police when they did arrive. Just because I'm young doesn't mean I'm a heartless fucker."

He motions for the kid to follow while walking away from the bodies and back toward the edge of the parking lot. They don't need to contaminate the scene any more than what they already have. Glancing around to see if anyone came outside to investigate the sounds of gunfire, he grimaces. No one appears to be interested.

"What's your name, son?"

A flicker of distrust sparks behind dark blue eyes. "Mason Hall. Yours?"

"Cooper Hollingsworth, Chief of Police in Malvern, Arkansas."

Mason cocks his head in curiosity. "You're a cop? No wonder you're such a good shot. You on vacation, too?"

"Yes, with my wife. You mentioned you've been calling the police for hours. Why?"

"My parents never came back from town. They left last night to see a show." A look of sorrow flashes across Mason's face. "I've got a wicked case of altitude sickness and stayed here. I gave up calling them when their cells went straight to voicemail. I thought maybe they had an accident or something, so that's when I started calling 9-1-1. Then, I watched the news and changed my mind about them having a wreck."

The dread in the kid's voice sends his hackles rising. "You mentioned the news earlier—what did you mean?"

"Man, I can't believe you don't know, being a cop and all." Mason puts his phone back in his pocket and replaces it with a cigarette. He lights up, fingers shaking.

Frustrated and cold, Cooper's temper sparks and just as he is about to give Mason Hall a piece of his mind, more gunfire breaks the stillness of the morning, followed by faint screams. He looks in the direction of the noise, cringing as the morning sun's rays bounce off plumes of dark, black smoke. Judging from the location, he assumes it is from downtown Steamboat.

Gunshots? Screaming? Fires? Where's the sirens? Where's all the emergency personnel? Shit. I need to overcome the rising sense of dread.

"Wife and I were hiking all day yesterday and into late evening. When we got back, we crashed. Made a rule about cell phones and TV—no watching, texting, surfing the net—while on our vacation. So no, I missed the news. What's going on?"

The expression on Mason's face shifts. His gaze fills with fear. "Bio attack of some sort. People are dying in droves all over the world. President Thompson was in the middle of a news conference yesterday morning, talking about what the government would do in response. He gave a nice little speech until several reporters went all nuts and attacked each other. It was a bloodbath for several seconds until the transmission ended. The emergency broadcast service came on right after, saying everyone's supposed to get to their local high schools for testing of some sort. Then bam! The screen went black, and the TV's been out ever since. Not long after, the net went down, too."

Karla appears on the walkway. "Cooper? You okay?"

"I'm fine, darling. Any luck getting through to the police?"

"No. TV seems to be out, too and I—"

Karla's comments are interrupted when the security lights go out.

"See? Told you the power's next." Mason mutters.

"Get back inside, Karla. Right now." He grabs Mason's arm and tugs. "Come inside with us."

Mason doesn't offer any resistance.

Once back inside the warm condo, Cooper ushers Karla and Mason into the living room. He addresses his distraught wife first. "Honey, I need you to keep calm. Something's wrong, like you said, and Mason here is gonna share all the information he has about the situation with us. Right, Mason?"

Mason sinks into the soft folds of the couch and nods. Karla's face blanches. Cooper knows she senses his own fear. Years of being the wife of a cop taught her to recognize dire situations.

"Mason? Start from the beginning and tell us everything you know. Don't leave any details out. Okay?"

"If you really want to know what's going on, watch this." Mason holds out his phone. "I downloaded two videos from the news before the internet died."

Cooper takes the phone with trepidation. Karla moves over behind him to view the screen. Taking a deep breath, his other hand instinctively finds his wife's. By the time they finish watching the disturbing videos, his hands tremble, and Karla softly cries.

"How fast can you pack, honey?" Cooper whispers.

"Five minutes and we're outta here." Karla's voice is thick with tears. She takes the stairs two at a time.

After handing Mason the phone, Cooper sighs. "Where's home for you, son?"

"Phoenix and Santa Fe. We alternate between the two for my dad's job."

"You're welcome to come with us. We could try to get you close to Santa Fe."

Tears glisten in Mason's eyes as he shakes his head. "I'm going to wait here in case my parents return."

"I don't think that's a good idea. Not after what we just watched."

"I really don't care what you think. I'm staying." Mason rises and walks to the front door. "If...*when*...they come back, and I'm not here, they'll come looking for me."

Cooper glances at the kitchen then back to Mason. He senses the kid won't budge, and he certainly has no right to make him. "Let me give you some extra food and water."

Mason opens the door and steps out. "No thanks. I've got plenty. Good luck, Chief. Hope you make it home."

"Stay safe, son." He watches the kid walk away before closing the door.

"Honey? The bags are ready. Help me carry them, please."

Without a word, he bounds up the stairs and helps tote their luggage down to the main floor. Karla is bundled in her ski gear, which will make additional packing difficult. "Let me bag up the food and water and then we'll head out."

Karla paces back and forth in front of the door. "Hurry, Cooper. I can't get in touch with Charlie or Charlene. Jesus, what's going on? Were those videos even real? How can they be? People were eating each other. That can't happen! Maybe it's a trick or something?"

Cramming the food and water into the big cooler they brought with them, he yearns to lie to his bride and smooth her frazzled nerves by telling her everything will be fine, and they'll be home soon, yet he cannot utter the lies. He's seen the real deal with his own eyes—even though he doesn't want to believe what he witnessed.

If he lies to her, she won't stay on guard and that might cost them both their lives.

"Yes, they're real. Those boys I shot looked just like the ones on the videos. And they attacked the girls and...well, just like in the videos. We'll talk about this once we're on the road. Stay here and let me load up the truck. Okay?"

"Hell no. I'm not leaving your side. Ever. We go together." Karla picks up a suitcase. "We can get all this in one trip. I want to go home. Now."

Cooper finishes with the supplies and brings them into the living room. He can tell by the look on her face she isn't going to change her mind. "Fine but let me go first. I'll get the suitcases and you grab the food. Ready?"

"I'm ready to wake up from this awful dream." Karla grabs the box of supplies.

"Hang on." He moves over to the window, clicks the key fob, and remotely starts the SUV. "Go straight to the passenger side and get in. Don't stop. Okay?"

Too frightened to respond, she simply nods. He picks up the two suitcases and motions for her to open the door.

The morning sun is bright and gives them plenty of light to see. As they make their way down the walkway and out to the parking lot, Karla gasps when she spies the bloody corpses. More random gunfire erupts in the distance and the screams intensify. Dark, thick smoke fills the sky.

"Dear Jesus." Karla whispers. "Please protect us!"

They make it to the SUV. He opens the back hatch and tosses the suitcases inside while Karla stuffs the supplies in the backseat. He looks around once more when the sound of footsteps crunching on the snow near the passenger side reaches his ears. Assuming Mason changed his mind and decided to join them, he shuts the door.

"Cooper!"

Karla's scream sends his heart rate sky-high. He moves too quick and loses his footing on the slick ice, landing hard on his ass.

"Oh, my God! Get away!"

Forcing his sore body to move, he stands, clinging to the bumper with one hand, using the cold metal as a safety measure. He gains steady footing and comes around to Karla's side of the SUV.

What he sees makes his mind gridlock for a split second.

All three dead girls are on their feet, only steps away from his terrified wife. Karla claws at the door handle, desperate to get away from the bloodied monsters heading her way.

"Open that fucking door and get inside!" he screams.

The sound of his voice cases the three women to turn their attention on him. They shift direction and lumber toward him, giving Karla a chance to open the door and slip into the passenger seat.

Yanking his weapon from his back pocket, he blows the heads off the already-dead three girls. After they each fall to the ground, he feels dizzy and sick at the same time.

This. Isn't. Happening. No way. I'm dreaming.

"Cooper! Let's go!" Karla yells from inside the SUV.

The terrified plea from his wife snaps him back to reality. He spins around, slipping and sliding across the pavement until reaching the driver's door. Once inside, he shoves the gear into reverse, tromps on the gas, thankful for the snow tires and four-wheel drive, and leaves the bloody mess in the parking lot.

Karla cries softly in the passenger seat. "So much for our Christmas and anniversary."

Cooper doesn't answer. He is too busy driving.

They make it out of the main part of town with only seconds to spare. Upon hearing the roar of U.S. fighter jets in the crystal blue skies above, he looks up in time to see wisps of smoke from missiles streak across the sky. The impact from numerous bombs makes the SUV shudder and shake as Steamboat Springs is obliterated.

By its own government.

The thought makes his stomach churn again.

***

The snow was thick and numerous times, Cooper nearly lost control of the vehicle after hitting patches of ice. By the time he and Karla arrived in the small town of Heeney almost twenty hours later, his fingers were numb from his death grip on the steering wheel. Karla had been catatonic after attempting several times to use her cell phone with no luck, and then listening to the EBS blare over the radio. Thankfully, once they entered the mountain passes, the radio went silent.

What they heard before it went static—and what they saw during their drive—terrified them both.

***

Now, he stands in front of the SUV he rented four days ago, his mind on the brink of shutting down. The entire town of Heeney is dark except for the solitary streetlight at the edge of the gas station they'd stopped at to refuel and use the restrooms. Shifting his gaze, he stares at the small storefront.

"You should've waited for me to clear the place, Karla. You fucking should've waited!"

He takes one final glance at his dead wife. The small bullet hole between her eyes, and the explosion of red behind her head on the snow, makes tears run down his face. He doesn't know much about what sort of biological contagion the world is dealing with, but what he does know causes his head to spin as he relives what happened less than five minutes prior.

During the drive, Karla seemed fine, yet the minute they arrived at the gas station, that changed. She got out and ran toward the building to pee while he yelled for her to wait, but Karla was afraid she couldn't hold it any longer. By the time he exited the SUV, Karla was at the front of the store. When she opened the glass doors, everything became blurred.

Four dead bodies lumbered out, groaning, moaning, lurching toward Karla. They moved fast and though she tried, she didn't have a chance to run far because one latched onto her leg and she went down.

Cooper had pulled his gun and fired, but in the middle of the melee, he missed the head of the one on top of her, hitting the shoulder. Karla's screams drove him to the brink of madness. The other three creatures closed the gap fast, so he popped them each in the head, dropping them in less than two seconds.

When he took aim again at the one on top of his wife, he was successful the second time, but unfortunately, he was too late. The creature had bitten a large chunk of flesh from her calf muscle.

He'd run to her side, yanking off his jacket to use as a tourniquet, wrapped her leg and tried to calm her, but she was in a complete state of panic. He finally convinced her to stop screaming and picked her up off the ground. He made it to the passenger door, opened it, set his wife on the seat, and then she screamed again.

"Cooper! Look out!"

He'd spun around, noticed another corpse at the back of the store, grabbed his weapon and fired.

Nothing happened.

He was out of bullets.

"Shit!"

He'd secured Karla in the seat then shut the door. His hands shook while fumbling around for the extra magazine in his jacket pocket. The frigid air numbed his exposed fingers to the point they were nearly useless.

He'd moved away from the SUV to draw the corpse away from her and it worked. After loading a fresh magazine, he fired., and the body collapsed in a heap less than ten feet away.

He'd run back to check on Karla, and that's when his life changed.

His once beautiful wife was gone. Black, dead eyes stared back at him, the lovely, sweet lips that used to kiss him with passion, were pulled back into a snarl. She'd jumped out of the SUV and landed on top of him, growling, hissing, clawing at his face.

Overcome with sorrow and shock, Cooper had no choice. His sobs were drowned out by the sound of gunfire as he blew a hole in his beloved wife's head.

"I can't do this now! Fall apart later!"

Refusing to dwell any longer on the carnage he created, he wipes the tears away. To bring his focus back, he slams his head into the metal doorjamb several times. The impacts aren't hard enough to knock him out, yet enough to ring his bell and clear his thoughts. With each smack, he repeats, "Charlie and Charlene. Charlie and Charlene. Got to get home and make sure my children are safe."

Smacking some survival sense back to the forefront of his thoughts works. It is stupid and a waste of time to stand outside, weeping and puking like a child. Though no longer young children, the twins are only twenty-two, and they need their remaining parent to keep them safe.

"Yeah, like I did such a good job of keeping Karla alive." With a final smack of his head, he dislodges the thoughts of incompetency by failing to protect his wife. "No, get it together and think. Stand out here any longer and I'll just attract more of those things. I'm the Chief of Malvern Police Department for God's sakes! I need to act like a man and move my ass!"

The SUV will require more gas to make it to his destination. He assumes a generator keeps the pumps and lights on since every other place previously passed didn't have any power. A click from the gas pump, signaling the tank is full, brings him out of the funk. After returning the nozzle, he pauses.

"Think. Calm down and think. Stop looking at what I just did and plan ahead!"

Knowing he has more than a thousand miles to go before making it back home to Arkansas—alone because he just shot and killed his lovely wife—he trudges through the snow toward the door to the station. He reasons if the power grid is down way up here in the mountains, it is probably down everywhere. Finding working gas stations along the way may prove to be impossible, so he decides to look for anything inside he can use to fill with fuel.

He welcomes the distraction—any distraction—to keep from going insane.

He finds four empty gas containers and takes them outside before returning inside and grabbing several plastic bags from the counter. With precision, he fills them up with water bottles, protein bars, cans of soup, and some cereal boxes until the bags are nearly bursting. Slipping out the door, he stows the bags in the backseat then turns his attention to filling the containers with gasoline.

Once the gas is put away, he struggles to walk away. The thought of leaving Karla's body behind makes him woozy. It is wrong to just leave her corpse in the snow, alone, without a proper burial. Charlie and Charlene would never forgive him.

Returning to the inside of the store, he scours the place, looking for anything suitable to dig a grave with yet finds nothing. The only thing of use is a snow shovel, and it certainly isn't strong enough to tear up frozen ground with, but he takes it anyway.

Stopping in front of Karla's body, tears stream down his face while grappling with the awful truth—he killed his wife.

"No, that wasn't Karla. It was just her shell. Her soul's gone to Heaven."

After looking around once to ensure he is still alone, he scoops shovelfuls of snow on top of Karla's stiff corpse, welcoming the flowing tears because they blurred the image.

Once finished hiding the monstrosity, he looks over at the others he shot earlier. Though they aren't human any longer, they once had been, just like his wife. Before they got sick from whatever the hell is in the air, they'd been loved by someone. Sons, fathers, uncles. It isn't right to leave them out in the open either.

It takes him almost twenty minutes to cover the bodies with fresh snow.

Satisfied he's done all he can, he sets the shovel down, saying a silent prayer for all of them.

For the world.

For his children.

For himself.

After climbing behind the wheel, he cranks the engine over. Without looking back, he eases out onto the main road, numbed by the events of the last twenty-four-plus hours. While driving, he wonders what fresh hell awaits him in Denver, and all the other major cities he must drive through to get home. On the drive from Steamboat, they hadn't passed a single, live person.

"No matter. I'm going to get my kids. Ain't no one gonna stop me, either. No one and nothing. Don't matter if I'm the last survivor. I'm going home."

"You aren't the last survivor, Chief."

Cooper nearly runs off the road. His foot automatically steps on the brake and the SUV slides across the road. Once it comes to a stop, he spins around and finds Mason Hall staring sheepishly from the floorboard.

Cooper is flabbergasted. "What…how?"

Mason tosses off the blanket he's been hiding under and climbs into the back seat, minding the full bags. "I snuck in while you were fighting off those girls in Steamboat."

Cooper stares at the frightened kid, noting his pale face and quaking torso. His first instinct is to rip the kid's head off for a variety of reasons, mostly from scaring the bejesus out of him seconds before, but considering what is going on, he is glad he isn't alone. "Why? I thought you didn't want—oh, never mind now. You should've announced your presence earlier. I sure could've used some help back at the station."

"When I left your condo and headed back to mine, I saw those girls move. I freaked and changed directions, deciding to circle around back and climb in through a window or something. I was crouched in the parking lot, watching them to see what direction they'd take, then you two came outside."

"Bullshit. You just didn't want to be alone. I get that. To be honest, I'm relieved. Felt sorta bad leaving you behind. Come on up here and help me keep watch. Phoenix is a bit out of the way. You got anyone in Santa Fe?"

Mason climbs into the front passenger seat, a big smile on his face. "My aunt and uncle. They stay at our place when we're in Phoenix."

Cooper turns the wheel and continues the journey. He waits a few minutes to speak, mulling their past conversation over in his mind. "What really happened to your parents, son? Seems to me they wouldn't have gone to a show, knowing the world was falling apart."

Mason's cheeks fill with blood. "You figured that out, huh?"

"Took me longer than normal, but yes. Cop, remember?"

"They did head into town, like I said, but it was early morning, right after the President's news conference." Pulling out a crushed cigarette, Mason sticks it between his lips. "They decided to go get extra food and water so we could head back to Santa Fe. I didn't go because I was too busy puking. The altitude sickness part was true. Sorry about your wife. Really. I wanted to help, but I was too scared. After it all went down, I thought, you know, you'd need some time to grieve before I made any noise."

Cooper feels a twinge of sadness for the kid. He is a grown man, pushing hard on sixty's door, and he is well past the point of sanity. Mason is just a boy so he cannot blame him for being scared. "Well, I've got two rules you'll need to follow while we make this trip. One, no smoking unless you roll the window down. That rule changes if any of those things are around. Then, the window stays shut, and smoking ain't allowed."

"And the second?"

"Don't ever lie to me. I've got a feeling we're gonna run into some major shit as we get closer to populated cities. I need to know I can trust you. Liars can't be trusted."

Mason's lips curve into a lopsided smile. "Done. Thanks for not freaking out and kicking me to the curb or yelling at me for not helping. Sorry I'm such a wuss. Computer nerd, you know?"

Cooper returns the smile, even though it is fake. "Break one of the rules, and I will. Now, stop yapping and keep quiet, Geek Squad. I've gotta concentrate on driving."

"I've had worse nicknames." Mason chuckles. "Call me whatever you want, I don't care. At least we're both still alive to speak and hear."

Cooper doesn't respond and keeps driving. *The question is, Geek Squad, for how long?*

Chapter 2 - Next Steps
Monday, December 22nd – 6:15 a.m. – Central Standard
Time

REED NEWBERRY AWAKENS to the sounds of an argument. Though the two grumbling voices are barely above a whisper, there is anger and fear in both. Before opening his eyes, he listens long enough to determine Turner and Jesse are in the middle of a heated conversation.

"You can't do that again, Jesse. Ever. It's too dangerous to go outside alone. You should've woken me up."

"Turner, I've already apologized twice and promised not to do it again. Besides, I wasn't alone. Shaun was with me."

"Only because he followed you. When you left, you thought you were alone."

"That's enough. Forgive me for not thinking straight. You didn't see your mother kill herself in front of your eyes. I did. Would've been hard enough to handle under normal circumstances, but we ain't anywhere near close to normal anymore. Drop it, Turner."

"I won't drop it. You're right—we ain't close to normal. What if one of those things was wandering in the woods or you ran into some military thugs my dad said are lurking outside? Shaun said you weren't even armed. Look, I get why you're upset. Really. And I'm so sorry about your mom. I can't even begin to understand how you must feel. All I know is I don't want to experience the same kind of pain from losing you."

Reed heard enough. After glancing over at Jane, who is still in deep sleep, he rises from the cot. It is time to intervene before Jesse snaps and wakes everyone by yelling at the boy. The cave is dark, illuminated by only a few candles strategically interspersed along the ground leading to and from the latrine. He wishes they were scented because the cave reeks. He figures they are beeswax or some other non-toxic material. As careful as the Addison family is about everything else, he doubts they'd risk their lives by burning toxic candles underground.

It takes several seconds for his vision to adjust to the darkness while making his way across the damp ground. The edginess in Jesse's voice makes him uneasy. She is just like Regina when angry. His heart clenches with grief just thinking about his sister.

Oh, God. Regina. What you did...what you sacrificed...I still can't comprehend it all. Can't grasp all this mess. The hole in my heart will never, ever heal. Poor Jesse. I'm really worried about her mental state. How long will it be before she cracks? Before we all do? How much longer do we each have?

Turner and Jesse stop talking when they notice him heading in their direction. Even in the dim light, he can tell Jesse's face and eyes are red from crying. The dark circles under her eyes make her look like she is high. Even from several feet away, he can tell she is antsy. She rubs her arms while pacing in front of the cot in small circles. He'd forgotten about Jesse's claustrophobia. Though he appreciated the shelter provided by the Addisons, he wishes it was above ground.

No, I wish none of this had happened and we were all back at home. Except there isn't a home to go to any longer. Those fighter jets obliterated all of Malvern. We barely escaped in time.

Before he has a chance to say anything, Walter appears at his side. "Turner? Need some help with the water outside. Can't seem to get the pump working. We all need to get cleaned up, and that ain't gonna happen until we fix whatever's wrong."

Turner squeezes Jesse's hand and places a light kiss on her dirty cheek. She smiles, but it is feeble fake as she watches Turner follow his father outside.

"You doing okay, honey?" Reed whispers.

Tears fill her eyes. Her hair hangs in tangled knots around her face. She looks like she's been on the streets for weeks. Poor thing shakes her head.

"I know, honey. I know. Try not to be so harsh on Turner. He's just worried about your safety. I am, too. What you did yesterday morning was—"

"Don't you start in on me too, Uncle Reed. There's too much running around inside my head, and I don't need another lecture to add to it. God, I can't stand it here. It's like being in jail all over again. I'm filthy, tired, sore, and jittery, on top of several other things. It's almost like I'm detoxing. Take me outside. Please? Just to walk around for a bit. If I stay inside here another minute, I'll flip. I can't do this. Can't handle being trapped."

"Of course. Let me use the bathroom first."

Martha clears her throat to announce her presence and puts an arm around Jesse's shoulders. "Reed, why don't you go and see if you can help my husband and son with the water pump? The faster we get it working, the faster we can all take hot showers. I'll take Jesse outside. I need to go get the remaining supplies from the vehicles we left behind and could use the help. How about a nice walk through the pretty woods, honey? That'll make you smile. Communing with nature does wonders for a troubled soul."

"Shower? A *hot* shower?" Jesse's mouth drops open. "Are you serious? How's that even possible?"

Martha smiles and Reed notices pride sparkles in her eyes. "Arkansas is full of hidden springs all over the state, just like the bubbling ones in Hot Springs. Granted, the water's too hot to actually bathe in when it comes straight from the ground yet considering how far it'll have to travel through plastic pipes to get inside here, it should cool off enough that our skin won't burn away."

"A hot shower. My God, I don't think three words have ever sounded so inviting." A fleeting memory of the last dual shower Reed took with Jane pops inside his head. There certainly wouldn't be any of that sort of private, intimate time now. Too many people around and no door in the shower. The small indentation carved into the rock serving as a place to get clean didn't even have a curtain.

Wow, still a dude. Thinking about sex in the middle of all this mess. Some things never change.

"There's a spring less than half-a-mile from here." Martha points toward the entrance. "It's another reason Walter picked this location. Took us six months to install a pump system underground and run the pipes through this thick rock. Guess since we ain't turned it on in years, its being stubborn. Don't you worry, girl. Once those boys get it up and running and you get under that warm water, it'll be just like home."

Jesse snorts. Reed can tell she is about to say something rude, so he puts his hand on her shoulder. "That's certainly good news, Martha. As I said the night we arrived, we more than appreciate your hospitality. I'm sure everyone's nerves will settle somewhat after a nice shower and change of clothes. Right, Jesse?"

Jesse shrugs Reed and Martha's arms off. "Yeah, right. I didn't have time to pack fresh clothes or go shopping for new ones at Walmart. It's the end of the world and I'm wearing pajamas. Classic."

"Don't you worry none about that, girl." Martha eases the tension with a gentle laugh. "I'll share some of mine stored away up here until we can snag you some new ones. Now, get your coat, honey. I'll meet you at the entrance. Oh, and make sure to grab a portable radio from the shelf by the door. Turn it to channel forty."

Jesse doesn't say a word in protest, she simply nods once and walks away, shoulders sagging as the weight of their situation bears down on her body. Reed and Martha watch her thin frame disappear as she rounds the corner leading to the front entrance.

"Sorry about that." Reed feels the need to offer an explanation. "Jesse doesn't handle enclosed spaces very well."

"No apologies needed, Reed. Ain't none of us handling this nightmare too well. She's doing fine."

"I don't think there were twenty words spoken by all of us yesterday. It was like everyone's battery conked out."

"That's because we all needed a mental break to digest what we've been through. I believe the proper term is shock. None of us were prepared for this. None of us."

"You and your family were."

"We were ready for troubling times, but this? Well, this never entered any of our minds. A bio attack: sure, we were ready for that, yet we always thought, you know, it would be a flu epidemic or something similar. A disease we'd hide from until it died out, then things would go back to normal. What's happened—well, ain't none of us ever took the whole dead rising from the grave serious, so trying to absorb the horrors of the last forty-eight hours is gonna take time. Lots of it."

"No, we surely weren't. Listen, Martha, I owe you an apology for what I said back on the road—"

"Don't." Martha holds up a hand. "After what happened with Regina, I'm surprised you and Jesse aren't still catatonic. Go, give Walt and Turner a hand. I'll take care of Jesse. She probably needs a female's soft touch. She'll just try to remain defiant and stoic around menfolk. She needs to let out what she's feeling then be done with it. I'll be more than happy to be the shoulder she falls apart on."

"Thank you, Martha. You're one hell of a gal. Walt's a lucky man. You sure Lamar or one of the deputies shouldn't go with you? For safety's sake?"

Martha pats the rifle slung over her chest. "I guarantee you, I'm a better shot than all of them. We'll be fine. Promise."

Reed smiles and walks to the makeshift bathroom. After relieving himself, he grabs his jacket, portable radio, and gun. He glances over at Lamar, Allsop and Bailey, who are all huddled together by the food pantry, whispering. Jane is still out on the cot. She'd spent almost the entire day before taking care of all of them, checking for any signs of contamination, dressing wounds, and lending a sympathetic ear to anyone who wanted to talk.

Most were still too preoccupied grappling with the traumatic events to speak.

He stops in front of Lamar and points toward Jane. "If she wakes up before I get back, will you tell her I'm with Walt and Turner, helping to fix the water pump outside? Don't want her to wake up and worry. Oh, and that Jesse is going with Martha to fetch the remaining supplies from the Humvees."

Lamar nods. "Sure thing. Want one of us to go with the girls?"

Though Reed doesn't know Lamar Wilson very well, he notices the man has changed during the last forty-eight hours. He guesses Lamar is close to his age, yet he looks a good ten years older. Hell, if he had a mirror and peeked, he probably does, too. All of them are worn down to their mental and physical nubs. "No, they'll be fine. Think Jesse needs some bonding time with another lady."

"Mr. Newberry, I'm so sorry about what happened with the Chief." Bailey's voice is full of emotion. "She was a great lady. A true hero, and none of us will ever forget what she did for all of us."

Hearing another man choke back tears makes Reed's heart pound with grief. He nods in agreement while swallowing the lump in his throat.

Bailey looks over his shoulder. "How about we follow them, but they don't *know* we're doing it? I don't like the idea of them going out alone."

Reed glances over his shoulder. Martha is busy checking the magazine on the AR-10. "I have the feeling Jesse's in good hands, so no. Need y'all to watch the place while we're gone. You know, in case...?"

He lets the words trail off, knowing it is an unnecessary sentence. They all are aware of the dangers. The three men nod and return to their previous conversation, so Reed exits the cave.

The minute he smells fresh air he realizes how smelly the cave had been. He would never admit it to anyone, but he understands why Jesse is having such a difficult time. Human beings weren't meant to live like moles.

Gravel crunches behind him. Stiffening, hand immediately reaching for his weapon, he spins around.

"Easy, big guy." Martha grins. "It's just us. We are off to get the supplies and clear our noses."

"Sorry," Reed lets out a huff of air. "Nerves."

"All of us are edgy, Uncle Reed. Some more than others."

Reed notices Jesse's holding a gun. The sight almost makes him laugh at the absurdity.

Jesse takes a deep breath of fresh air. "Guess we'll need to start announcing our presence before one of us snaps and shoots before knowing what's making the racket. Don't forget to watch out for others, Uncle Reed. The guy I ran into yesterday probably ain't alone."

A sense of unease crawls up his back. The faint smell of smoke in the air tickles his nose. Seeing his niece holding a rifle makes his stomach burn. Jesse doesn't have much experience with any sort of weaponry.

"Stop looking at me like that, Uncle Reed. Ms. Martha's gonna teach me how to shoot. I'll make Mom proud."

He considers saying something funny to ease the tension, yet nothing humorous pops into his mind. "Sorry. Been worrying about you my whole life. Some habits never die."

Jesse smiles for the first time in days. A real, genuine smile that tugs at his heartstrings. The grin spurs memories of only days before, when Jesse rushed around getting ready for work, constantly on her phone either texting or talking to Turner. The smile reminds him of the normal life they once lived.

And how they never would again.

"Reed, got your radio tuned to channel forty?" Martha inquires.

"Yes."

"Good. The spring's about half-a-mile that way." Martha pointed to the west. "Follow their footprints. We'll be back soon."

"Be safe, sweetie. You, too, Martha." Reed swipes a kiss on Jesse's cheek. "See you soon."

Martha and Jesse turn and head down the trail. The first rays of the morning sun filter through the trees, providing them with plenty of light. Though the temperature hovers near the freezing mark, the crisp air helps clear the clogged images inside his head. He watches their backs until the trail turns and he cannot see them any longer.

Following the steps made by Turner and Walter, he scans the dense forest for any signs of movement. The stillness in the woods is eerie. No birds chirped. No sounds of forest creatures scurrying around, busy searching for their morning meals. No squeaks or noise from bugs. He wondered if whatever disease afflicting mankind affects other living things, too.

The thought makes him shudder.

Less than three days prior, the inhabitants of the planet went blindly about their daily lives, just as Reed, Regina, and Jesse had done. People filled their moments alive with trivial, mundane bullshit; some more than others. All the ridiculous obsessions with vapid, surface-level crap are over. No more breaking news with the latest celebrity gossip. Not another program full of self-proclaimed political experts vying for attention to get their messages heard across the airwaves. No plastic-riddled celebrities living extravagant lifestyles from the hard-earned money of the middle and lower-class groups of citizens.

No one will worry about getting enough rest after a long day slaving at work, just to get up and do it again, day after day, until their bodies give out. No panicking about low funds in the bank, or whether enough money has been squirreled away for retirement. Those out of work searching for an income before they lose everything and find themselves on the streets—over.

Those still alive and already are trapped in a world gone mad.

The abundant worries of the world were over in one swoop. Now, those who'd survived the first purge only had to concentrate on living another day. Finding food. Shelter. Weapons. Society was now free from the constant bombardment of meaningless drivel, but he craved those mindless distractions because the new world they are in sucks.

Big time.

Stopping at a large outcropping of boulders to his left, he pushes the thoughts of the past away. The beautiful view of the Ozark National Forest is tainted with plumes of gray smoke languidly floating on the light breeze. Turning to look south, he notices most of the smoke wafts from the direction of Little Rock and Conway. Though he cannot see any flames, he knows the cities lie in ruin, just like Malvern.

Unaccustomed to hiking, he decides to catch his breath while staring at the vast forest. Walter had done a fine job finding a secure, off-the-grid location to hole up in. They had food, water, medical supplies, weapons, a surgical nurse, bedding, and soon, apparently hot water. All fine and dandy things to have, considering what they are facing, but the question of how long jackhammers inside his head, vying for complete and total control. How long, really, do they have? A day? Week? Month? Years?

The thought of living inside the cave for an extended period makes his head thump.

Though he'd only given a cursory glance at the first night they arrived, he wonders how long the staples will last. Even though Walter and Martha had prepared for a disaster, he doubted they counted on having so many mouths to feed and clothe or the vast supply of bullets they'd need to keep the dead at bay.

His mouth goes dry. They are safe now since the walking monstrosities are far away from their location.

Temporarily.

If things continue to go downhill, the dead will eventually run out of food and start shambling around the hills and mountains looking for more.

How long can they, realistically, last underground? How long will it be before they succumb to the disease? Other than being bitten or scratched, they had no idea how the sickness is transmitted. Is it possible they are immune, and if so, are there others like them? Ones scavenging for food, shelter, water, a fucking life?

Why didn't the government prepare better for the disaster? His stomach jerks into a knot, assuming the government is at fault and did a piss-poor job of containing whatever unspeakable hell they'd unleashed.

What will they do when the food runs out, or someone suffers a major injury? Even if some miraculous solution to those problems manifested itself—like the good ol' U.S. Government got their shit together and cleaned up their enormous cluster-fuck—what then? Were they all doomed to spend the remainder of their lives surrounded by rock? Go back to—literally—the era of the cavemen and devolve?

"I'd offer you a penny for your thoughts but seems a waste. Money don't mean shit anymore."

Reed jerks at the sound of Kyle Pender's voice. "Dammit, Kyle! That's twice in less than twenty minutes my heart rate's spiked to dangerous levels. Surprised it hasn't exploded yet."

Kyle steps out of the shadows of the trees to his right and joins him. "Sorry. Figured you heard me walking up."

"No. Guess I just learned a valuable lesson. When outside, it's not a good idea to start thinking about things. Gotta concentrate on the surroundings. Pine over shit when underground."

Kyle leans back against a boulder. "No doubt. Nice scenery, huh? Well, except for the smoke and the eerie stillness in the woods."

"I'll take this view over what we've seen recently."

"Agree." Kyle holds out a bottle of water.

Reed nods his thanks and takes a long gulp. After finishing, he casts a sideways glance at the former cop. "You doing okay?"

Kyle shrugs a set of beefy shoulders. "About as good as you look, I suppose."

"Well, that ain't good, because I figure I look like hammered shit."

"Yeah, you do. We all do."

Reed blows out a huff of air. "What're doing out so early?"

"My mom always used to say that there wasn't a better way to clear your head when full of sorrow than walking in the woods. Said the trick was to soak up all God made and realize how small we really are compared to the vast expanse of what He created."

Reed tamps down the smart retort dancing on the edge of his tongue. Though not exactly an atheist, he never really gave much thought to a higher power. Then again, the anger swirling around in his mind, and the outburst directed at Pastor Trent, gives him pause. Why, if he didn't believe, did he curse the man upstairs for allowing the world to fall apart?

Instead of responding with a negative comeback, knowing Kyle did attend church regularly, he decides not to broach the subject of a deity. Besides, he knows Kyle is grieving for Regina and doesn't need to add any more stress on his shoulders. "Did it work?"

"Hell no. Just pissed me off more. All I could think about was all the things I didn't say to Regina when I had the chance. Now, it's too late."

"She knew, Kyle. I know my sister better than anyone. That's why I knew about you two without her telling me. Twin bond, you know?"

"Yeah. She talked about that a lot. Said it was like you lived inside her head sometimes. She didn't tell anyone about us because she worried about how you and Jesse would take the news."

"That woman never worried a day in her life about how I'd take anything she did. Regina's only concern was about her daughter. After going to all those counseling sessions, listening to them docs yak her ears off, they had her so paranoid about how to handle Jesse, Regina couldn't see straight."

"I agree about that part. Whenever I'd bring the subject up about letting our little not-so-secret relationship out, she'd start spouting about how addicts don't handle change well. Frustrated the shit out of me. I wanted to shout from the rooftops about how I felt about her, but she wouldn't let me."

The heavy emotion in Kyle's voice, only there because he obviously loved her, is painful to hear. "She loved you, too. Never seen her so happy, even when she was married to Fred. He was a good man and he loved her, but he wasn't Regina's equal. She wore the pants in the family, so to speak. You? Well, you made her stronger, pushed her buttons, urged her to strive toward greater things."

Kyle's mouth gapes open. "How do you know that?"

"Because she finally learned to cook."

"Regina wasn't exactly the homemaker type, that's for sure. Thanks for telling me, Reed. I appreciate knowing she was happy with me. Shit. What am I supposed to do with this now?"

Kyle shoves his hand down deep into his pocket, extracting a ring. Reed's stomach drops. "Really? Oh, damn. When?"

"Had it all planned for Sunday night. I made dinner reservations in Hot Springs at her favorite Italian restaurant."

"Bella Arte?"

"Yep. Following dinner and plenty of wine, the plan was to go see the lights at Garven Woodland Gardens. I was going to pop the question by the forty-foot Christmas tree. It was time we took the next step…"

Kyle's voice fades away. Reed stares at the ring clutched in his dirty fingers. Kyle tenses, lifting his arm over his head. Before he has the chance to chunk the ring over the cliff, Reed grabs his arm. "Don't. Not now. You're too upset. If it still feels right later then by all means, let it go. Just...not now. Okay?"

Kyle takes a deep breath. Reed feels the tightness in the man's shoulders ease. "Guess you're right. It's the last piece of a normal life I've got left. Been carrying it around like some stupid fool ever since I bought it, afraid I'd lose it."

If Reed doesn't walk away, he'll fall apart. Regina would have loved the simple, yet elegant ring, and looking at it, knowing it will never grace her finger, makes his heart pound with grief. He gives Kyle's shoulder a rough slap then starts walking. "Was on my way to help Walter and Turner with the water pump so we can all take us a hot shower. We *all* need to get off the last two days' worth of funk. Could probably use some help."

"Of course."

Reed hears him sniffle twice while they make their way up the twisty trail. After a few minutes of silence, Reed whispers, "She'da said yes. No doubt."

The crunch of Kyle's footsteps behind him stops. Reed continues forward, unwilling to turn around.

"I'll catch up." Kyle mumbles. "Call of nature."

Nodding, Reed keeps going, blinking back tears. Kyle's voice had cracked with emotion, and he knew the man needed a minute or two alone to compose himself. Reed isn't a sentimental kind of man, but considering any minute could be their last, he felt Kyle deserved to know Regina really did love him.

I would have gladly called you my brother, Kyle. Gladly. Hey sis, you watching from up there? Did you see that? Kyle bought you a ring! He wanted to marry your stubborn ass. Chief Pender sounds nice, doesn't it?

Reed's internal thoughts vanish when the sounds of another argument up ahead reaches his ears. This time, it is Turner and Walt snapping at each other. He is too far away to catch the words, but the angry tones ring across the valley.

Kyle comes up behind him. "Sounds like someone woke up on the wrong side of a cot this morning."

"Yeah. Guess they forgot we should be grateful for the chance to wake up another day. Come on, let's get in between them before Walt loses it. He's running on fumes."

"Ain't we all?"

Reed and Kyle pick up the pace, rounding the curve of the trail just as Walt yells, "Turner? What the hell are you doing?"

"I see something down there. Oh, shit!" Turner screams.

Reed and Kyle run faster, making it just in time to see Turner's legs disappear over the edge of a cliff.

Chapter 3 - Stuck in the Mud

Monday, December 22nd – 7:15 a.m. – Central Standard Time

EVERETT STOPS WRITING as footsteps approach the door. Chill bumps burst from his skin, wondering if Kevin, or one of the others, has come to end his life.

"Doc? Got a minute?"

"Of course." He is thrilled it is Dirk and not someone who wants to pound his face to a pulp.

Dirk opens the door and steps inside. Everett notices he's shaved and changed clothes. He needs to do the same, but he's been so wrapped up in researching, he's neglected his own personal hygiene.

"Time for you to take a break and eat." Dirk crinkles his nose. "And please reacquaint yourself with soap and water. You're kinda rank, Doc."

Heat filles his cheeks. "Yes, I'm aware. You know it's bad when you can smell your own scent. Just trying to tie up some loose ends."

Dirk stops about ten feet away, glancing over at the notes. "We all appreciate your dedication, Doc. Really. However, since we're sharing living space down here, and there really isn't much ventilation, we all need to make the effort to remain clean. Come one, the rest of the gang went topside. The shower's all yours."

He moves to the other side of the room, grabs a suitcase, removes a fresh pair of pants, underwear, shirt, and socks, and finally turns to face Dirk. "Thanks for watching out for my safety. Part of the reason I've remained in my room is, well, you know. I figured out of sight, out of mind."

Stepping back to the door, Dirk steps into the hallway. "I think you've overestimated how we feel about you, Doc. Yes, Warton is still upset, but he's cranky with all of us, too. It's not just you. He's not handling what happened with Porterfield well. Can't really blame him. They've been friends for a long time and went through some heavy shit in Afghanistan together. They were more like brothers than friends. Being forced to kill someone you care about isn't easy to recover from."

"I can't even begin to understand the depth of his pain." Everett follows Dirk down the hall. "I hope I never have to."

"You might, considering any or all of us may turn up sick. If that happens, you'll have no choice but to shoot. That's the way of the world now. Kill, or be killed."

"Yes, then reanimate."

"Again, that's where you come in, Obi. You've had your head buried for the last two days. Any new developments? Ideas? Epiphanies?"

"The sticking point right now is the fungi. They've always been a virulent pathogen, destroying more species than all others combined. Scientists have identified over seventy-five thousand different fungi species, yet some researchers recently suggested in papers their actual numbers may be over the one million mark."

Dirk groans. "That's comforting to know. Is that why you're having such a hard time with your own research?"

"Yes. For one, I only have access to the few books I had on hand here. Without the ability to search the internet, or communicate with other scientists, it's kind of like looking for a needle in a haystack."

"Because you can't narrow down which particular fungus was inside Porterfield, right?"

"Correct."

Dirk furrows his brow. "I don't understand. Aren't you a microbiologist? Isn't this like, your forte?"

"Yes, which is why this is so damned frustrating. I've never seen this species before. I've looked through all the books I have until my eyes crossed, but no luck. Until I can figure out what species it is, trying to create an antifungal will be impossible. Besides, I'm going to need more than what's inside Porterfield to manufacture its opposite."

"Why? I mean, it's just a bug, right? Can't bugs be killed?"

He almost laughs until realizing Dirk is serious. "Fungi are not insects. They aren't animals or plants, either. They do share some common traits with us, such as breathing oxygen and getting energy from ingesting food. Both humans and fungi are eukaryotes."

"Doc, remember, English please? Dummy this down for me."

"Oh, sorry. The cells of fungi and humans are very similar. Each has a nucleus and organelles, which are enclosed in membranes inside each cell, and responsible for carrying out certain biological functions. We also have in common similar sets of genes and cellular processes."

"So, what exactly does that mean, Doc?"

"Let me come at this from a different angle. Have you ever had athlete's foot or knew anyone who did?"

"Yes. Had a wicked case of that shit years ago. Thought I'd never get rid of it."

Everett smiles, glad to have found common ground. "Exactly! The reason why it's so difficult to kill off a fungal infection is because of the similarities in the cellular structures. When attempting to kill the fungus with an antifungal, oftentimes, the side effects in human cells are disastrous. Tissue death usually occurs."

"Aren't you full of good news."

"Hey, you asked. Don't shoot the messenger."

They both stop at the door leading to the small, community shower. Dirk takes a deep breath. "Let me see if I can grasp all this medical mumbo-jumbo. The fungus in Porterfield isn't a strain—"

"Species."

Dirk narrows his eyes, clearly annoyed at the correction. "What's in Porterfield isn't a *species* you're familiar with, and to plan an attack strategy against this mess, you need to know exactly what sort of fungus you're dealing with. Right so far?"

"Correct."

"And even if you do find out what type of species this thing is, it might not matter, because killing it just might kill the infected person? Well, they're already dead, but you get my drift."

Everett nods, watching as Dirk absorbs the disturbing truth.

"So, basically, you're saying were fucked?"

"No, not completely. This fungus didn't retreat into a spore, which is good news for us. Usually, when under attack, they do. When that happens, fungi can live outside of their hosts without food for long periods of time. However, the fungi inside Porterfield did not do that. The other strange thing is all the cells converged in the brain, rather than the lungs, like most fungi."

"Does that mean the disease isn't airborne?"

"Correct, and that is a good thing for us. As I mentioned before, transmission only occurs through an exchange of bodily fluids, or ingestion of something tainted with the fungi. The other thing bothering me is I don't believe this particular species is native to the United States. Based on its structure, I'd say it's from someplace with a moist, tropical environment. I've never seen anything like it before. That, however, is just an educated guess at this point."

For a few seconds, Dirk chews on his bottom lip while staring at the ceiling. "You mentioned earlier you needed more of the fungi?"

"Yes. I'll need quite a bit to create—"

"An antifungal. Got it. So, guess this means when the guys return, we'll need to decide who's going to go get more specimens."

The sound of Warton and the others walking down the hallway set Everett's nerves on edge. The other men are big and burly, as is Warton, yet none of them hold the animosity toward him like Kevin does.

"Breathe, Doc. Warton's not a rabid dog."

"I beg to differ. Think I'll go take my shower now just in case he aspires choking me to death again."

Kevin rounds the corner, the rest of the men behind him. They all looked tired and edgy. Kevin gives a stern look at Everett before turning his attention toward Dirk. "We've got company. Found four Humvees about three miles away."

"Any signs of their owners?" Dirk queries.

"No, but the vehicles have been driven recently. The girl and man I ran into yesterday morning mentioned they fled Malvern, and the military gave the orders to terminate all citizens. Judging by the items inside, the Humvees weren't driven up here by grunts. I'd bet money the girl and her friends took them. There's no telling how many people were crammed inside those four beasts, Dirk."

"Let's just keep an eye out for now. Most likely, they are trying to survive, just like the rest of us."

"Yeah, well, maybe so. Maybe not. I say we don't take any chances at this point. It's time to go bury Porterfield's remains and then get the hell outta here."

"And go where, exactly?" Everett inquires, immediately regretting the words.

Kevin grimaces. "I wasn't talking to you, Berning."

"Enough. Both of you. Doc, go and take your shower. Kevin, I'll help you put Thomas to rest, and then you and I are going to have a long chat."

"You can flap your gums all you want, Kincannon. Doesn't mean I'll listen." Kevin storms down the hallway. The other men follow in silence.

Dirk waits until they disappear. "Again, ignore him, Doc. I'll handle Warton, you just concentrate on a thorough spring cleansing. There's soap and shampoo in a small bag next to the sink. Use it. Maybe getting rid of the grime will give you a new perspective on the situation. A clean body and mind may unleash some hidden ideas."

"Ah, if it were only that easy." Everett sighs. "We, uh, aren't going to head back to Dr. Thomas' place, correct? Not that I enjoy living underground, but we are safer here."

"We aren't going anywhere until you get a handle on things. Well, I'm going topside with Warton to help with Porterfield, but other than that, we're hanging here. How long depends upon you and your big brain."

Dirk walks away, leaving Everett in a stunned funk by the door. Bearings finally back in place, he steps inside the bathroom and over to the shower.

While shedding his stinky clothes, he replays the entire conversation with Dirk. The weight of the situation bears down on his soul like a ten-ton piece of steel. "No pressure. None at all. Dammit!"

Once under the stinging spray of the hot water, his thoughts wander over to what he hadn't told Dirk. He knows the former soldier is a smart man and guessed it wouldn't take him long to grasp the enormity of the situation.

Yes, he needs to figure out what species of fungi they were dealing with and obtain more to create an antifungal, however, it will be used as a proactive measure on those who'd yet to contract the disease or administered to someone immediately after contamination.

Those who'd been infected with the mass of fungi inside their brains controlling them like marionettes, don't stand a chance. Brain tissue will die, too, if a cure is created.

There isn't any hope for healing the undead. The world will never be the same—what ls left of it. Does he really want to stick around, watching the last remaining vestiges of humanity disappear? Is the entire infrastructure of civilized society on the verge of collapsing?

That's what is on the horizon. With no power, things will decay at a rapid pace. One thought keeps poking its way up to the forefront of his mind no matter how hard he tries pushing it away.

Nuclear power plants.

He tries to recall how many cities have nuclear reactors and seems to remember reading somewhere the numbers are close to sixty in America. How many are around the world? The thought makes him shudder. Thank God Arkansas only has one in Russellville, which is a little over a hundred miles away.

If the power grid is down for the count and radiation leaks out, how long will it be before the entire globe is covered in radioactive waste? Did the employees of the plants lock themselves inside when shit hit the fan? If so, how long will they stay, manning the facilities, changing out the moving parts due to metal fatigue? Will they leave when food runs out, or they simply cannot take being entombed?

He says a silent prayer, hoping the power plants had some sort of fail-safe mechanisms in place to slowly shut the dangerous facilities down in the absence of human caretakers.

Unable to stand thinking about a nuclear disaster any longer, he turns his thoughts over to Porterfield. It was one thing to see a human turn into a monster on a screen yet quite another in person. The sickness destroyed any semblance of humanity in Porterfield, leaving behind nothing but an empty shell controlled by vascular connections. A shudder of fear ripples throughout his chest. How would he handle being topside and coming face-to-face with one still reanimated, interested in nothing except eating him?

No ability to reason; no moral compass; no way to communicate.

Oh, he knows what he'd suffer a major stroke or heart attack before getting one whack in. His stomach sours.

When Dirk and the others grasp the news about the finality of the outbreak, will they allow him to stay underground with them? Will they continue to offer protection, or force him to leave? What if one of them snaps and kills them all?

The biggest question: Does he want to remain living in a world with no hope?

He stares at the wet razor sitting on the ledge. A faint whisper inside his mind urges him to pick it up, slice through the brachial artery, and bleed out while enjoying one last shower.

Hand controlled by the suicidal thought, he reaches out and snatches the razor. Studying it, he feels around with his fingers, finding the artery. Just one, painful and deep slice, will end the nightmare.

No more worrying about things. He can slip away into the next phase of life amidst a torrent of red. Join his family on the other side, stop all the terrifying thoughts from controlling every minute of his life. Atone for his colossal mistake.

Suddenly, he recalls the remainder of the conversation between Dirk and Kevin.

They were going to bury Porterfield, which is a huge mistake. Porterfield's remains need to be burned. It is the only way to make sure his body is no longer a threat to the rest of them. If any of the fungi are still alive, it is possible they could leak out and contaminate the ground.

That vanquishes the thoughts about slicing his arm.

He tosses the razor to the floor. "Can't keep blaming myself for something I didn't do. Someone else made these monsters, not me. Enough wallowing in this pit of sorrow. I'm still here for a reason. Time to figure out why. I can't waste another minute worrying about what-if's. I've got to stop them before they bury Thomas."

***

"Warton; Winters. Follow me, please."

Kevin looks up from his perch on the chair, immediately glowering at Dirk while chomping on a protein bar. "May I finish eating first?"

"It's portable." Dirk struggles to keep the irritation in his voice at bay. "We need to give Porterfield a proper burial. Doc is finished with him."

Clive Winters rises and joins Dirk at the door. The youngest of their group at only twenty-eight, Clive is also the largest. He looks like a combination of wrestler and linebacker. Clive is a quiet man who follows orders without batting an eye or questioning them. Dirk brought him onto the team after the soldier's young wife overdosed on heroin while he was deployed overseas.

"Do we need to suit up?" Clive asks.

"Doc told me earlier we won't get sick unless bitten or scratched, but just to be safe—"

"Or get fucked up." Kevin deadpans while rising to his feet.

Dirk shoots him a dirty look. "Suit up, boys. The rest of you keep trying the radios. See if you can raise anyone. If you do, make sure not to give out our location. Understood?"

"On it, sir." Drake Denton replies. "I know the drill."

Dirk steps back out into the hallway. "Stay sharp. Eyes on the lookout at all times. If Dr. Berning asks, tell him where we went, and that we'll be back shortly. Then, after we chomp some grub, we'll all need to sit and listen to what he's learned during the last forty-eight hours."

"Joy."

"Buck up, Warton. According to what Doc told me earlier, you'll get a chance to release some of your pent-up anger. Soon. He needs more specimens."

"Of course he does. Sick bastard." Kevin moves ahead of Dirk. "Mad scientists always do."

Dirk shakes his head while bringing up the rear. He hopes once Warton has a chance to say his final goodbyes to Porterfield, the nasty demeanor will change. If it doesn't, and Warton continues holding animosity toward the elderly scientist, things will get even more uncomfortable inside their little slice of Hell on Earth.

Ten minutes later, all three fully covered in bio suits and Porterfield's nasty remains encased inside a body bag, Dirk, Kevin, and Clive carry the former soldier topside.

None of them speak while trudging through the quiet forest. Dirk silently replays the entire conversation with Everett, unable to shed the overwhelming sense of guilt weighing heavy on his chest.

The minute Dr. Berning mentioned Laredo, something inside his mind snapped. Visions of the night he snuck in and rescued the old codger made his skin crawl. With full clarity, he recalled Dr. Berning attempting to grab the satchel with the vials and formula, yet in the heat of the moment, Dirk yanked him away.

There was little solace in the fact he didn't realize at the time what little bombshells were inside the bag. He wished Dr. Berning would have insisted they retrieve them. Though it would have been dangerous, he would have turned around and headed back.

No, he wouldn't have. He would have brushed it away and convinced Dr. Berning it didn't matter, and they needed to live, not die for some lab chemicals and he could simply create more.

Though he had no clue who the men were in the vehicle that had chased them that night, he knew enough. Daryl Riverside had been working for some lowlife thug, probably a drug lord from south of the border. After Dr. Berning retold their last words to each other and related all their conversations as Daryl drove to Laredo, there was no doubt about where Riverside's loyalties resided.

Someone wanted the cure enough to kill people for it and used it to create a nightmare. Whether their intention was to destroy society or not, it didn't matter because it had.

Dirk tried to salvage the remains of the computers, hoping he'd be able to pull some information off the hard drive or server, but no luck. Riverside was smart and made sure to completely wipe them before physically destroying them. Rather than risk an electronic trail leading back to his doorstep, he didn't attempt any searches on the internet about Riverside. Instead, he waited and scoured news sites for any articles about a dead body on the outskirts of Laredo.

The only article, a brief blip in the *Laredo Morning Times*, surfaced two weeks after the incident. There had been no mention of a body, or the vehicle, when the charred remains of the small cabin were discovered.

There had been an active case opened because the fire was ruled arson, and only a one sentence blurb about spent shell casings found at the scene. The article hinted that the cabin was likely used as a drug drop or perhaps a hiding spot for illegals crossing the border.

No articles about the subject ever surfaced after the initial write-up, and he concluded the thugs sent to Laredo returned to the scene, snatched Riverside's body, took the truck, and set the place on fire. Obviously, they took the serum and research notes with them, too, and handed them over to someone with dark, evil intentions.

As much as he desired it not to be the case, he had no choice but to come to terms with the face he played a major role in the current nightmare. Way more of a part than Dr. Berning. Though he'd kept the ugly truth to himself, he realized he had no choice but to come clean to the others. It was time they stopped blaming the nightmare on the old man and put the mistakes behind them. They needed to work together as a cohesive unit to survive.

Shaking the depressing thoughts away, he focuses his attention back on the present. The final resting place of Thomas Porterfield looms ahead. His stomach sours, recalling the two days he'd spent, alone, retrieving and burying the twenty-seven others the year prior.

As the trio arrive at the small glen, full of twenty-seven mounds of dirt with no markers, all three men remain quiet.

Are they each thinking the same thing he is: *That could be me. Soon.*

Without being instructed, Clive and Kevin ease Porterfield's remains to the ground next to the last grave. Dirk walks over, shovel in hand, and starts digging. Clive and Kevin join in, filling the morning silence with the sounds of digging.

Since the ground is hard and nearly frozen, the process of digging a shallow grave takes almost fifteen minutes.

They lower Porterfield's body into the hole. He removes the bio suit and tosses it on top of the body bag. Kevin and Clive do the same, and they all work in tandem to fill the hole with dirt. "Kevin, would you like to say something?"

"Already said my goodbyes when he was still, you know, him." Kevin shakes his head. "What's in the ground isn't my friend."

"Can't argue that point. Let's head back and see if Denton's had any luck with the radio."

Snorting, Kevin mutters, "You've always been a glass half-full kinda guy, Kincannon. Me? Well, I've gone from glass half-empty to ain't no water left at all."

All the men freeze when hearing someone tromping through the woods from the direction of the lab. On instinct, they reach for their weapons.

"Stop! You can't bury him!"

"Shit, what is the mad scientist doing here?" Kevin asks.

Dirk lowers the rifle. "Doc? What are you talking about?"

Everett stops at the tree line to catch his breath. "The fungi! You can't bury him because of the fungi!"

"We don't take orders from you, old man." Kevin stiffens. "Besides, we already did."

Signaling Warton to be quiet, Dirk heads toward Dr. Berning's position. Warton and Winters follow. He lowers his voice so only the other two can hear him. "If he's out here, alone, and unarmed, there's a mighty good reason why. We need to find out what's on his mind, so let me do the talking."

"He's crazy, and yet you want to give him a chance to—?"

"Enough, Warton. Enough. That's an order."

Kevin bristles at Dirk's instruction yet remains silent as the trio join Dr. Berning.

"Okay, Doc. Explain."

"Thank you, Dirk. To kill the fungi completely, it must be burned. Burying it exposes it to the ground."

"Don't worry, Doc. We put him inside a body bag."

Everett sighs. "That's not going to be enough. Over time, the fungi will—"

"How much time?" Dirk interrupts.

"Weeks. Months. Depends upon the type of fungi and other factors."

Dirk motions for Dr. Berning to head back toward the cave. "Then let's worry about that later. Right now, we need to concentrate on the present, not worry about the what-if scenarios of the future. Okay?"

"But—"

"No buts, Dr. Berning. This was a discussion that could have waited until we returned or happened before we left. You risked your life coming topside without a weapon, and that simply cannot happen again. We need you to remain healthy and in one piece. Now, let's get back to the lab and have our little pow-wow."

The ominous tone works. Dr. Berning lowers his head and follows orders.

"Like I said before, you're a glass-half-full guy, Kincannon, and the rest of us know there ain't a drop of water left."

As the four men walk back toward the lab, Dirk tries to figure out the best response to Warton's words.

He has squat so he remains silent while they trek through the forest.

I'm right there with you, Kevin. Right there with you.

Kevin snaps his fingers. Dirk, Everett, and Clive stop in their tracks, each turning around. The man is rock still, his head cocked right. The foursome holds their collective breaths, each listening for any foreign sounds.

After a full minute, Kevin shakes his head, motioning for them to continue forward. Dirk nods toward Clive and Everett, and then walks over to talk with Kevin. "What did you hear?"

Kevin glances back toward the glen. "Swear I heard radio chatter. Must be losing my mind or slipping back into my days in Afghanistan. You didn't hear anything?"

"No, but if you say you did, I have no reason to doubt you. We already know we aren't alone, so let's hope it's just one of the survivors you encountered yesterday. Probably out searching for food."

"That thought doesn't worry me. What puts me on edge is thinking the soldiers followed them here and plan on wiping them out. We need to hurry and get back to the lab. My gut tells me something's wrong."

"Then let's move." Dirk turns and jogs up the trail. The others sense the urgency, even Dr. Berning, and follow.

WALT WATCHES IN horror as his son slips and tumbles down the cliff from about twenty feet away. Turner's screams are muffled as his body bounces and rolls over the boulders and ground.

"Turner!"

Running full speed, he doesn't even slide to stop at the edge. Bracing his hands behind him for traction, dirt and rocks exploding under his feet, he goes after his boy. The sound of Turner's body slamming into the ground makes his stomach lurch. The first two tumbles Turner grunts and groans with each impact, but when he quits making any noise, he fears his heart will stop.

"Walt! Wait!"

Ignoring the voice of Reed above him, Walt keeps his focus on Turner. The mountainside is steep and rugged, full of large boulders and jagged shale. The scenery whizzes by in a blur as he slides down the treacherous terrain. Up ahead, he sees Turner's body flip about ten feet into the air then land with a final, hard thump at the bottom of the cliff.

"Son-of-a-bitch!" Walt mumbles under his breath. "God, please don't let my boy die."

Time crawls at a snail's pace as he maneuvers his body down the slope. By the time he reaches Turner, he realizes he isn't moving. Even from ten feet away, he can tell Turner's right leg is broken.

Reaching his son's side, he kneels, heart thundering in his chest. Turner is a bloody, broken mess. His leg is bent underneath his back at an odd, unnatural angle. Cuts and gouges pepper his face, arms, and neck. A four-inch gash over his right eye split the skin, and it looks like his nose is broken.

Small wisps of steam stream from Turner's nose. Walt almost yelps with joy. His boy is still alive. Yanking off his gloves, he gently pats his bloody cheek. "Son? Son? Can you hear me?"

No response. Turner is out cold.

He looks up at the sound of someone coming down the slope behind. Kyle Pender is less than twenty feet away. He's never been so glad to see a cop before. In seconds, Kyle slides to a stop next to him.

"Reed went to go fetch Jane. Is he okay?"

Walt nods, turning his attention back to Turner. "Leg's broken, along with his nose. That last boulder knocked him out. We're gonna have a hard time getting him outta here and back to the cave. That's a good fifty-foot drop."

Kyle glances around, studying the terrain. "Looks like there's a glen about twenty yards ahead. The incline isn't as steep as this one. Probably will take longer to reach the cave, but at least we'd be able to carry him without having to wrangle some rope and pull him out."

Walt opens his mouth to answer, but the sounds of footsteps crunching through dry leaves make him clamp it shut. Using hand motions, he signals Kyle. The cop's reaction was immediate. Kyle pulls his weapon from its holster, training it in the direction of the noise.

Both men crouch lower, listening to the sounds draw closer. The glen is surrounded by a thick tangle of trees and boulders, so he cannot make out who—or what—is heading their way. Straining his ears, he picks out three, distinct footfalls. Judging by the steady rhythm, they aren't dead.

Relieved they are dealing with humans rather than reanimated monsters, his heart rate slows for a split second but spikes again when three bodies appear at the edge of the glen, all dressed in full bio suits and carrying a body bag. His gut rumbles in disgust. *I knew it! Government tools!*

Kyle seems to understand the gravity of the situation. With slow, controlled movements, he holsters his gun, replacing it with the rifle. Careful not to make a sound, Kyle moves to the prone position, barrel aimed at the intruders. Walt holds up a hand to wait. Though he hates the idea of not blowing the bastards' heads off when they have the chance, he doesn't want to risk it. There might be more hiding in the shadows. Even if Kyle takes out the three men, the gunfire will draw out any others lurking about—or worse, give away their presence to any dead corpses shambling around—and they cannot run away fast enough carrying Turner's unconscious body.

Kyle's hands move in strange patterns. It takes Walt a few seconds to recognize the motions. *The man knows sign language? Hallelujah!*

Kyle signals, *"I won't shoot unless they spot us or head this way."*

"Good. Looks like they just plan on burying someone. Probably one of their buddies. They wouldn't risk being outside to bury some unfortunate civilian they killed."

"Agreed. You were right all along, Walter. Wonder where they're holed up? Hopefully, not close by."

"See those other mounds? This ain't their first trip to the makeshift graveyard. Their camp's gotta be close."

For the next few minutes, Walt and Kyle focus all their attention on the three men. His heart pounds, worrying about how long they have before Reed returns with Jane. He is almost glad Turner is out cold, because if awake, the boy is just klutzy enough to give their position away.

The thought immediately makes him feel like an ass, but it is the truth. They wouldn't be here, crouched against the cold, hard ground holding their collective breaths like scared prey, had Turner paid more attention to the surroundings. How many times had he warned him to be careful near the cliff's edge? Too many to remember. Martha is going to rip him a new one when they return after seeing the damage Turner's fall had on his body. He dreads seeing the anger in her eyes and hearing the accusations spewed in his direction borne from a mother's worry for her only child.

No one can rip a person apart verbally better than Martha. When angry, she is a force of nature. Mild Martha morphs into Molten Martha. That's the nickname he secretly bestowed on his wife the first time he saw her in full riot mode.

Thoughts of Turner's predicament, his wife's reaction, the cold ground, worry about noise giving their position away from Jane and Reed, vanish when the men ease the body bag into the grave. They each removed their white bio suits. His blood runs cold when he recognizes one of them as the man he followed in the woods—and lost—the day prior.

Kevin Warton.

The men are talking now, but he cannot make out the words. Blood pulses inside his ears as anger overrides his thoughts. He wants to kick himself for losing the man's trail. Any doubts he had about Kevin Warton being in the military are all gone.

Barely able to contain himself from giving Kyle the signal to shoot, he concentrates on memorizing the other faces and body structures. He knows, without a shadow of a doubt, they'll run into each other again.

Once Turner was back at the cave and safe, he plans on having a long discussion with the rest of the group, setting out his plans to find—and wipe out—the government bastards lurking in their territory.

The sound of another's footsteps crunching through the leaves catches his attention, followed by a male voice yelling, "Stop! You can't bury him!"

One of the men yell a response, then the first man replies, "Because of the fungi! You can't bury him because of the fungi!"

The three men turn and walk up the hill out of earshot. He tries, yet cannot make out, the rest of their conversation, though he can tell it is heated. After a few minutes of back-and-forth, the men head west. Neither man speaks for an additional few minutes after the foursome disappear.

"That was close." Kyle whispers.

"Too close. Wish we could've heard the rest of the reason why the old man was in such a tizzy about burying the body. Did he say fungi?"

"Yeah, he did. Do you think he meant fungus?"

A fleeting memory of prepper meetings surfaces. "Fungi is the same as fungus, so same thing."

"God, I hope that means they ain't still contagious after death. Or, shall I say, their second death?"

"Fungal. Makes sense. No wonder the government wanted to burn the bodies. Well, that little spectacle did help us in some ways."

"Agreed. We know there are at least four, they're armed, obviously military, and their camp is that way." Kyle nods west with his head. "And they didn't seem to be concerned with covering their steps, so tracking them should be a breeze."

"Exactly. In fact, I think we should—"

His comments are cut short when the radio on his hip crackles to life.

"Walt? We've got ropes and Jane's here. Want us to head down?" Reed asked.

Turning around, Walt looks up, spotting Reed and Jane standing at the edge of the cliff. He shakes his head then answers on the radio. "No. We'll secure his leg down here and circle back. Maintain radio silence. I mean it. We ain't alone."

Reed waves in acknowledgement, so Walt turns the radio off. "Damn good thing they didn't come back while those grunts were within hearing range."

"No shit. I'll need your rifle to use as a splint, so unload it please. We'll use this to secure it with." Kyle offers up his belt then removes his jacket and shirt. He rips the shirt in two and immediately wraps the material around Turner's bleeding skull. "You should let me handle this."

"No, I can do it."

Kyle puts his hand over Walt's. "Didn't say you couldn't, I said you should let me. He's your son, and though he's out right now, the pain will probably wake him up. You cover his mouth to muffle the screams. I promise, as his father, you don't want the memory of knowing you caused him so much pain. I got this."

Walt hesitates. "You…know how?"

"Yes. Cop and trained paramedic. Remember we lived in a small town. People had multiple roles. Now, use the other half of this shirt and hold his mouth and head."

Scooting over until he reached the top of Turner's head, Walt remains quiet. His fingers tremble while he rolls the material into a ball and places it over Turner's swollen lips. Just as he leaned over to get a firm grip on Turner's shoulders, his son awakens. The terror and pain in those big, beautiful eyes tear his heartstrings into pieces.

In a flash, he removes the cloth. "Listen to me, son. Don't say a word. We ain't quite alone out here. If you understand me, nod your head once." Turner does, so he continues. "You broke your leg. Before we can move you, Kyle's gotta set it in a splint. It's gonna hurt like a son-of-a-bitch, but you can't scream. I'm gonna put the cotton back into your mouth. You bite down on it all you want, but no sounds. Can you do that?"

Turner closes his eyes. Tears leak from the corners. He nods again and opens his mouth. Walt secures the cloth and gently covers his lips.

"I've gotta move your leg out from under you first, then set the splint." Kyle whispers. "I'll move as fast as I can. On the count of three."

Turner opens his eyes again, locking gazes at Walt. "You can do this, son."

"Okay, here goes part one. Turner, can you roll to the left a bit?"

Turner groans while shifting his weight. Kyle works fast, pulling his right leg straight. Tears of pain erupted from his son's eyes.

"Good job, son. Okay, on the count of three. One...two...three!"

Turner's body tenses as it vibrates with a muffled scream. Even after all the years in the military, watching boys die in front of him, listening to them cry for their mommas with final breaths, he never experienced the kind of sorrow Turner's yelp of pain brought. Hearing— and seeing—his son in such agony, makes a lump of tears form in the back of his throat.

Turner's anguished screams stop. Walt realizes he is out cold again. The pain had been too much for his mind to endure, so it shut down.

"Well, the good news is the breaks are clean. Didn't penetrate through the skin." Kyle offers.

"Breaks?"

"Yes, Walt. I'm sorry. Turner broke both his tibia and fibula, which means he ain't gonna be walking, even with a cast or brace, for quite some time."

Walt's fights off a wave of dizziness. "How long?"

"That's a question for Jane, not me. In my opinion, just from this quick observation, three months."

"Shit." Walt mutters. "Can't think about that now. Will you check the woods through the scope one last time before we haul him outta here?"

"You bet." Kyle hefts the rifle to his shoulder. Squinting, he takes his time and scours the woods. "We're good. You ready?"

"Yep."

They ease Turner into the sitting position. After securing their bodies, they hoist him into the standing position.

Walt sighs. "This ain't gonna work. Not in this terrain. Too rocky. Here, let me take him."

"You sure? No offense, but my back and knees are younger."

"Positive. I'll need you to take point anyway. Guide me through this mess. Now, help me get him on my back."

In seconds, Turner's body firmly secured on his back, Walt and Kyle head to the glen.

After the first ten minutes of pulling uphill, his back and legs throb, but he refuses to give in to the temptation to switch places with Kyle, no matter how much his muscles beg him to change his mind.

Twenty minutes later, he has never been so glad to finish a hike. Reed and Jane are waiting at the edge of the trail. The sky is a dark, ugly gray. Snow clouds twist above them; a few snowflakes flutter around in the light breeze. Thankful the weather waited until he was off the trail to take a turn for the worse, he smiles.

Turner wakes. "What's going on, Dad? Why are you carrying me?"

Walt stops and eases Turner off his back. The words sound odd since his lips are swollen, but he doesn't care. He's overcome with gratefulness his boy is talking and at least making sense. While toting him through the woods, he'd worried Turner might have suffered damage to his brain from the fall. "Because you got your mom's balance, not mine. Took a nasty tumble over the cliff and broke your leg. Don't you remember?"

"Oh, yeah! I saw something down at the bottom of the cliff, Dad. Looked like shallow graves. I was trying to get a better look, then everything kinda goes blank after that. Glad I don't remember bouncing down the hillside."

Kyle steps over, draping one of Turner's arms around his shoulder. "Boy, you certainly are one lucky kid. You fell over fifty feet. Guess that thick skull of yours came in handy. Saved your little brain from getting cracked open."

"Your humor sucks, Kyle." Turner retorts.

"All of you hush." Jane grouses. "You can pick on him later. Right now, we need to get him back to the cave so I can fully care for all his wounds."

"Jane, does my wife know?"

"No. She left with Jesse earlier to go get more supplies. You're lucky too, Walt. I'll have time to examine Turner and get him cleaned up before his mother comes back. If she sees him looking like this—"

"Yeah, I know. She's gonna flip her lid. Ya'll might wanna stay outside when she returns. My wife's got quite a temper."

"Holy Mother of God! Turner! What happened to you?"

The sound of Martha's voice cuts through Walt's chest like a hot dagger. Under his breath, he mutters, "Shit," before turning around to face the only person in the world he fears.

"Baby!" Jesse chirps from behind Martha. Both women run full speed up the trail to their position.

Kyle leans over and whispers in his ear, "Not one, but two pissed off women heading your way. I sure am glad I ain't wearing your boots."

***

"You know, I expected an ass-chewing. Had myself all prepared for it, but I gotta say, the silent treatment is worse."

Martha stiffens at Walt's words yet doesn't turn around while continuing to stir the soup heating on the small cook stove. He moves closer, resting his hand on her shoulder. "Lover, please? Talk to me. Say your peace and let's get past this. Okay?"

Turning around to face him, Martha's eyes are backlit with fury, jaw twitching. He can tell she is fighting the urge to rip him to shreds. She swallows several times. "You didn't do your job, Walter. You failed."

"Martha, he's a grown man, and I can't keep an eye on him twenty-four—"

"I know that!" Martha hisses through clenched teeth. "I'm not talking about today's incident."

Stunned, thankful she whispered rather than yelling at the top of her voice, he cocks his head. "Then what are you talking about? How did I fail him?"

"You bullied that boy from the minute he was old enough to understand words. Scolded him for not being tough and rough like you. Mocked him about his interests in design, art, playing games."

"I—"

"No, don't you interrupt me, Walter Addison. You wanted me to talk, so I am. Saying things I shoulda years ago. You were ashamed of our son because he wasn't a jock, didn't have any interest in the things you did. That boy's feared your shadow ever since he was a toddler. All he's ever done his whole life is try living up to your ridiculous expectations of him and look what happened. Every time he'd come close to succeeding, you never gave him praise or any congratulations. Your pathetic compliments were always back-handed digs. By the time he was a teenager, you'd mashed his spirit to the point he didn't care anymore. He quit trying because he knew he'd never live up to your standards!"

Anger flares inside his gut. "That's not fair, Martha. I've always loved Turner."

"I never said you didn't. I said you failed him. Had you taken a softer touch, made yourself more accessible to him, he woulda paid more attention and *learned* rather than *mimicked* your actions, and I wouldn't be so freaking terrified, knowing my son almost died today. Not only that, but he's now basically immobile *during the middle of the end of civilized society*. What happens if we must flee here? Or one of those moving corpses finds its way to the cave?"

"That's what guns are for Martha. And since we're discussing the well-being of our son, recall you were going to leave without him the day the world went to shit. Why are you so freaked out now?"

That was the wrong thing to say.

Martha's face turns bright red as tears fill her eyes. "You best leave me be, Walter, and let me cool off before I say something I regret. I think you need to keep your distance at least until our son can walk again. I'll be busy taking care of him like I always have."

"Martha Louise, that ain't fair. Okay, I'll give you the fact I wasn't the greatest father. I tried my best. Truly. What happened today wasn't because I didn't love our son enough. It happened because he *did* use the skills I taught him and caught something I missed. Of course, that's when your genes kicked in and his balance failed. You can be mad at me all you want, but considering the way things are now, I don't think that's such a grand idea. Aren't you the one who said we should all stand together, keep each other safe, and pull together as a unit?"

"Don't you dare try and use my words against me."

"Why? You're willing to use my actions, or lack of, against me."

For a split second, he thinks Martha is going to hit him. So many emotions blaze across her face he feels dizzy. Instead of balling up her fist and letting him have it, she drops her head. Her shoulders bounce up and down as quiet sobs wrack her body.

Martha Louise Addison rarely cries. He cannot remember the last time he'd seen her fall apart. Seeing her so distraught makes tears of his own swell. He pulls her into his chest. "Oh, lover. Turner's gonna be okay. We're gonna be okay. I swear."

"Don't make promises you can't keep, Walter." She whispers between sobs. "Just…don't."

Something inside his mind breaks free. If they are going to make it, and keep each other safe, there can be no secrets between them. They'd all have to expose true thoughts, worries, feelings, and any information they'd been hiding to function as one unit.

He'd been hiding what he'd seen in the woods, and the fact he'd followed Jesse and Shaun. Now, he needs to come clean, stop pretending that he can handle things covertly, on his own, without sharing with the rest of the group. He also needs to confront Jesse about the drugs, and the reaction of Kevin Warton when he thought she'd taken some.

Inside the dimly lit cave, while the rest of the group huddled around Turner's cot, Walt clings to his wife, offering her all he has, which is only his love. "You know me, lover. I don't make promises I don't intend to keep."

Martha pulls away and wipes her tear-stained face on his sleeve. "And I don't cry over nothing. I'm scared, Walter. Scared."

"Me, too, so we'll just use the fear as fuel to make ourselves stronger, okay?"

She nods.

"Now, about that order to stay away?"

"I didn't mean it. You know how I get when mad."

"Good. Because I've lived my whole adult life by your side, Martha Louise. Don't intend on living out the remainder of it shut away from you. We need each other. More than ever."

"I know. I was just blowing off steam."

Leaning down, he kisses his wife, long and hard. She returns the kiss with passion. He pulls away before forgetting all about the others. "You're the last one who hasn't taken a shower. Go, get yourself under that hot water. It'll help ease the tension in your back and shoulders. I'll finish this here soup and make sure our boy eats it all."

"Thank you. I love you. Sorry about losing it. Guess it was just my turn."

He shoos Martha toward the latrine. "Get yourself all clean and soft, then later, we can figure out a way for both of us to ease the tension in our muscles."

Martha grins while shaking her head. "Even with the end near. Men."

He watches her make her way through the cave, stopping once by Turner's bedside to check on him. Reed rises and heads toward him. Turning back to the soup, Walter smiles, grateful his ass cheeks are still in one piece.

"From across the room, it looked like you dodged a bullet." Reed teases.

Walt chuckles. "Yeah, she let me have it but then forgave me."

"Don't take it personally. Mothers get like that when their chicks get hurt. Lord, I can't tell you how many times I saw Regina lose it over the years."

"I know, and I didn't. How's Turner?"

"Fine. Half of Rockport's fawning over him like he won the lottery. Plus, Jane gave him a hefty dose of morphine."

"How's Jesse taking all this? Should I expect her to get all emotional and freak out on me, too?"

"I don't think she'll leave his side long enough to give you a piece of her mind."

"Well, that's good to hear. Not sure I could stand having two women losing it in one day on me. So, while you're here and everyone else is out of earshot, got something to run by you."

"Shoot."

"Once we all finish eating, we need to have a group meeting. Got some things I need to share about a few items I've been keeping from everyone. While in the middle of getting my ass reamed by my wife, I decided it was time to make some changes. Come clean about certain things. Like Martha said—we all need to work as a group. Can't really do that if each of us is running in different directions."

"Well said. Couldn't agree more, but why tell me now? Why not wait until you address us all?"

"Ain't telling you what's on my mind, just that there's something on it, and giving you a heads-up in case you've got something you need to get off your chest."

"Oh, gotcha."

"I'm gonna ask everyone to be honest with each other and work as a group. If we don't, we'll get picked off one by one. It'll probably be like popping a boil: painful, stinky, and full of nasty goo, yet once drained, feel much better."

"Nice analogy to use before we eat."

"Hey, I said I'd changed my mind about some things, but not all. I still enjoy making folks cringe sometimes with—oh, what does Martha always say? My inappropriate humor? Yeah, that's it. Inappropriate humor."

Picking up a tray of plastic bowls, Reed laughs. "I can see why Turner hates jokes. If I'da grown up listening to that kind of humor, my funny bone would be gone, too. Don't worry about talking to us all, Walt. We've got each other's backs now. Since we're stuck in this cluster-fuck together, may as well make the best of it."

Chapter 5 - Proposals

JESSE ONLY LEFT Turner's side once to take a shower and change clothes. Looking down at the gray sweats Martha gave her earlier, she almost smiles. Though ugly, they are warm, clean, and certainly smell better than the tattered pajamas she'd worn for two days. Martha's superior planning skills included soap, toilet paper, and deodorant. The only thing missing is tampons, which makes sense. Martha Addison is way past the point of having periods, and probably didn't think there would be someone hiding out with them who still experienced the monthly mess.

All that was fine and dandy, yet seeing Turner's injuries broke her heart. She's always loved him yet the emotion intensified the moment she saw all the blood on his face. While observing Jane tend to him earlier, she forgot all about her claustrophobia. She watched Jane and Martha work on him, absorbing all their movements and how they handled his leg, broken nose, and gashes. Though they didn't have the proper materials to use as a cast to immobilize Turner's leg, they improvised. Walt broke down one of the cots, using the thick material and strong pieces of metal as a makeshift cast.

While watching, all she could think about was how lucky she was Turner was still alive, and they were surrounded by people who knew how to handle themselves. Yet, the biggest worry rolling around in her head was the injury. The broken leg left Turner helpless, dependent upon the rest of their small group for survival.

When she was in the shower—dear God, the *hot* shower—she was bombarded with memories about her mother's final moments alive. How she'd snuck in her feelings, veiling the comments under the guise of urging Marian to not give up. Enforcing the point home that Jesse was strong, and all the other snippets of love. She clung to the words inside her mind, using them as fuel to keep her going. When the dark, ugly images of her mother's last moments on earth tried to surface, she pushed them down deep, refusing to let them take control.

The time she'd spent on the streets, doing unspeakable, wretched things to survive long enough to earn money to buy another hit, came in handy. Back then, she taught her mind to ignore the vile, disgusting acts by pretending she was on the set of a movie, surrounded by actors. Forced herself to believe the pain and humiliation were make believe, and in the end, she'd win awards from adoring fans around the world for her spot-on performances.

Using the same tactics now to keep herself from going stark-raving mad, she simply pretends she is a cast member of a zombie series. One with an enormous set, and her family is home, watching her performance on television, marveling at how real things seem.

All her family, including Mom—her biggest fan.

The idea is silly and pathetic, but it doesn't matter. She will do whatever necessary to keep from blowing a mental gasket.

While walking with Martha to the Humvees earlier, the conversation was full of sweet, encouraging maternal advice, she realizes she was blessed. Though not her mother, Martha Addison is more than a suitable substitute.

Turner squeezes her hand. "You doing okay, baby?"

"Of course, I am. Because you are."

Turner smiles. It looks weird and painful. Between the bruises, swollen skin, and bandages on his face, it almost looks as if he is wearing a mask. Jane had given him some sort of medicine to help with the pain, so his pupils were barely visible. It is the first time she's ever seen him high, and it is quite strange.

"No, I mean with the cave. You haven't been outside in hours. Do you need to get some air?"

"Lamar said earlier it's snowing, and you know how much I hate the cold, so no. Besides, your fall seemed to cure my claustrophobia."

"At least something good came outta tumbling around like a runaway boulder."

Walter stands and clears his throat. "Okay, folks. It's time to have a come to Jesus meeting."

Shifting positions, Jesse settles in to listen. A twinge of worry pokes inside her stomach. *What now?*

"Where's the organ music?" Kyle teases.

Walt ignores the comment. "We have a lot to discuss this evening, so please bear with me as I tackle each item. Okay?"

The memory of her mother's speech at Walmart creates a lump of tears in Jesse's throat. Turner must have sensed the connection. He squeezed her hand again. "I love you."

She pats his shoulder. "Love you, too, you big klutz."

Walt clears his throat again, this time a little louder. "I ain't gonna rehash what we already know, but I am gonna add a few new twists we've learned recently. Recall on our way up here, I found evidence I assumed belonged to military personnel. After the events of the past two days, it ain't an assumption any longer."

"How do you know for sure, Walt? You see someone?" Mike Bailey asks.

"Yes, but before I get into that, let me finish. Things ain't gonna get better, at least not in the foreseeable future. We're on our own, and ain't no help on the horizon. We all witnessed the government's response. Our hometown, as well as the other big cities we passed through, are gone. If the decision was made to take out cities here in Arkansas, it's not too far of a leap to assume the same thing happened in bigger ones."

"Let's hope not." Shaun mutters.

"Trust me, Shaun, I don't want that to be the case, but we must look at the cold, hard facts here. We also need to come to grips with the fact that the dead, and the government, ain't our only enemies. Since things have gone to shit, those still breathing will do whatever is necessary to survive. Food, water, weapons, and shelter are what's at stake."

"Agreed. People ain't nice under normal circumstances. As supplies dwindle, so will their humanity." Lamar adds. "Hell, things were bad even before this shit happened."

Walt nods. "Yet another reason this cave was our choice for a beta location. The average citizen wouldn't dream of seeking shelter here, only other preppers. Don't think we'll need to worry about others like us now, though. I'm sure they're holed up in their own respective hideaways. The ones we need to worry about are the loners, civies, and grunts alike, scouring and scavenging to live another day."

Pausing to take a drink of water, Walt scans the room. His gaze stops on Jesse. For some reason, the look makes her stomach churn.

"I led off with those comments because they underscore what I'm about to say. We need each other, more than ever. There's not gonna be a rescue; this is the way our world is now. Whatever biological hit us may peter out, like most eventually do. However, what it left in its wake, namely, reanimated humans, won't disappear."

"No, they'll just increase as more people die."

"Unfortunately, I believe you're correct, Lamar." Walt sighs. "Martha and I did a lot of planning, but we didn't account for this many to be hiding out with us. We also didn't take into consideration we would never be able to return home. On that point, we sorely miscalculated."

"No one could have prepared for this." Martha adds, clearly trying to offer support. "No one in their right mind, at least."

Walt lets out a bitter chuckle. "Yeah, a zombie apocalypse was only discussed as an off-color joke during prepper meetings. This morning, I did some calculations. What we've got stored here food wise, if we ration wisely, will last about three months. While we don't have to worry about water since it's coming from the ground, we do need to think about how to replace the rest of our supplies. Long-term planning is needed. Think crops, livestock. We aren't the only ones who'll be out scavenging to survive. It won't take long until there ain't nothing left to find."

Jesse feels sick to her stomach. Walt's words sound like he plans on staying—living—in a cave.

Forever?

No. Fucking. Way.

"Wonder how many are even left?" Reed asks.

"There's no way to know unless we venture out and start counting heads. Ain't none of us interested in that dangerous op. We've only been up here less than a week and suffered a major injury, which depleted a large chunk of our medical supplies. Ya'll need clothes, too, along with other items. Finding more will require a solid plan to not only locate them but bring them safely back here."

Turner tugs Jesse's hand, urging her to come closer, which she does. "He's a real ray of sunshine, right? If I didn't know better, I'd swear he's enjoying this. Don't worry, babe. I'll build us treehouse once my leg heals. I know you can't handle living here forever."

"Turner? Did you have something to share?" Walt asks.

Jesse doesn't like the tone in his voice.

At all.

"No. Just trying to lighten the mood a bit, Dad. All this doom and gloom—"

"It's reality, son. Harsh, ugly-as-shit, reality. Ignoring what's going on in the world now will just cost us later."

"I know, Dad. We all know. Sorry, didn't mean to interrupt. Just trying to make Jesse smile."

"Mighty kind of you, son, and leads me to my next point. With the way things are now, we can't afford division or strife between us. We must work together to live. No secrets, no hidden agendas, no distrust. We all must know the person standing next to us has our back, one hundred percent."

"Of course we do, Walt." Reed nods in agreement. "That's how we all ended up here."

"For the trust to deepen, and continue, things need to be laid bare. If you see something, have an idea, a worry, comment, whatever, speak up. Don't keep things bottled up, thinking you can handle them on your own. There is no 'you' any longer. It's all about 'we.'"

A low rumble of whispers spread throughout the group. Jesse's hair stands erect. A heavy sense of foreboding pounds insider her chest.

"So, I'll go first with what I've been hiding. As I mentioned earlier, we ain't alone. Kyle and I ran into four government men today while they were burying a corpse in the woods. We counted twenty-seven other graves, which means they've been here a while."

"How do you know for sure they were military?" Shaun's brows furrow. "Did they see you, too?"

"Because of the clothing they wore and the weapons carried. And no, I'm confident they didn't know we were there."

"That don't mean shit. Look at us. Some of us are carrying military weapons and we all rode up here driving their vehicles!" Lamar throws his hands in the air. "Hell, a few of us even wore their clothes, and we ain't government grunts."

"True. However, the man I followed in the woods yesterday morning, certainly is. His name is Kevin Warton, and I heard him mention he was ex-military. He's also one of the foursome Kyle and I witnessed wearing full bio suits and burying someone today."

Jesse's mouth drops open. She casts a sideways glance over at Shaun, wondering if he mentioned their conversation with Kevin in the woods to Walt. Shaun looks just as shocked as she feels. He shrugs his shoulders.

Walt notices and stares directly at Jesse. "I believe you have something you need to come clean about as well, Jesse?"

Shocked by the revelation, her mind gridlocks.

"The only way you could know about that man is because you were following us, Walter." Shaun's voice is taut with anger. "The question is, why?"

"The important question is why didn't you tell us the entire story upon your arrival, Shaun? That's what I'm talking about here. We cannot, under any circumstances, keep secrets anymore! See how they turn on us in mere seconds?"

Jesse finds her voice as anger bubbles up from her chest. "You want the truth? Okay! Here goes. Hi, I'm Jesse Parker, a former meth addict. I'm also claustrophobic, and recently witnessed some fucked-up shit. My mother blew her brains out to save the lives of others, and I'm having a difficult time digesting all the shit I've seen in the last forty-eight hours. In the middle of a panic attack yesterday morning, I freaked and went outside to clear my head. Started thinking about all I've lost. Tried to convince my brain none of this was happening, because dead people walking around eating others ain't real! So, I ran. Found the pack we'd passed before on the way here. I opened it, and low and behold, my personal demon stared back at me."

"Oh, Jesse, you didn't?"

"No, I didn't, Uncle Reed, but only because Shaun stopped me before I had the chance. Yes, I would have given in to the temptation. I'm an addict. Trying to handle this mess sober is just too much. Too fucking much. But again, I didn't." She pauses and wipes away tears. "Shaun and I—we both suffered major losses in Malvern, so we decided to have a private service for Mom, Marian, and their baby. That's when Kevin Warton appeared from out of nowhere."

"And mentioned something during the course of the conversation you should've shared with us before, right?"

Jesse's anger ignites into an inferno at Walter's interruption and condescending tone. She lets go of Turner's hand and rises. "Really? You're giving me shit about that? Since you know his name, that means you were close enough on your little stalking mission to hear all our conversation. You've been keeping it to yourself, too. Hello, pot. I'm kettle."

"Enough!" Martha yells. "Secrets are out in the open now, so move on to the core issues! Stop going for the jugulars like those dead bodies roaming the planet."

"Kevin's demeanor changed the minute he thought Jesse took some of the drugs. I remember now." Shaun whispers to no one in particular.

"Walt, why in the world does that matter at this point?" Jane asks.

"Every bit of information we learn from here on out, matters. Every bit."

"Hell, maybe it wasn't even drugs Jesse found. Maybe it was whatever covert, secret shit the government concocted that started all this." Lamar interjects. "You're damn lucky you didn't try any, girl. Damn lucky."

"Good point, Lamar." Walt nods. "We know we ain't alone up here, and whatever the substance Jesse found in the bag sent this Kevin Warton into a tizzy."

"It was coke." Jesse offers. "No doubt."

"You said you didn't—"

"I didn't, Uncle Reed. But it was close enough. Trust me, I know."

"I just remembered his last comment." Shaun snaps his fingers. "When he was walking away, he said, 'don't do drugs.'"

Jesse rolls her eyes, angry with the entire conversation, biting her lip to remain quiet.

"So, there's another little morsel of information we can use." Walt's voice is calmer. "As we collect intel, we must share it, even if it seems trivial. Today, after three of the men, including Warton, buried the body, another came bursting through the woods. He was yelling at them not to bury it. Mentioned fungus."

"Fungus?" Jane looks scared. "Are you sure?"

"Yes." Walt answers. "Actually, his exact words were 'You can't bury him because of the fungi!'"

Jane rises and paces the floor. Jesse notices the same worried look on her face like at Walmart. "This isn't good. Not that it was before, but this is worse."

"Why?" Kyle asks.

"If this mess is from some sort of mutated fungal infection, there's no way to stop it. A lot of fungal infections are airborne, too. If the men you saw wore bio suits around a dead corpse—"

"Then all of us are at risk of getting infected? If it's in the air? Dear Jesus!" Shaun's voice cracks. "Boy, howdy, I wish I had a bottle of whiskey—oh, sorry, Jesse. Whisky's my personal demon."

"I'm a junkie, not an alcoholic." Jesse shoots back.

"Former, sweetie. Former junkie." Turner adds.

"Keep on topic, people!" Walt's voice booms off the cave walls. "We ain't trying to stop it, Ms. Jane. We're just gonna try to survive around it. However, I'd like your professional opinion and expect an honest answer. Okay?"

Jane nods while continuing to pace, gnawing on a thumbnail.

"We've all been around others who were contaminated. Hell, I believe at least half of us had blood splatter on our clothes. If this mess is airborne, why haven't we turned sick yet?"

"I'm not a doctor, Walter. I don't know. Maybe we're immune. Maybe this fungal infection isn't airborne. Some aren't. All I know for sure is, I've never seen—or heard of—any fungal spore that could turn people into the things we've seen. Ever. However, if that man you heard earlier—"

"Kevin Warton." Walt interjects.

"Warton, right. Don't really know what to make of his strange reaction toward Jesse and the powder. I don't believe that should be our biggest concern. If he was worried about burying a body, that ain't good, and we should be worried, too. Whatever this is, fungal, bacterial, viral, it doesn't matter. What matters is simple: can it cross species, and can live without a host in the ground?"

"There's only one way to find out those answers, Ms. Jane."

Jane's eyes widen in shock as she stares at Walter. "You want to find those men, don't you?"

Walt nods. "Yes. They'll be able to answer our questions. Give us an understanding of what's going on, what to look for, and how to stay free from exposure."

"You sure you ain't the one who fell and bumped his head today, Walt?" Lamar's tone is teasing yet tinged with disbelief. "Because if those men truly are from the government, they ain't gonna offer up shit. They'll just do like the others wanted: shoot us dead."

"I agree, one hundred percent. This time, we turn the tables. We'll stalk them, ambush 'em when they ain't paying any attention. Force them to answer our questions. Tomorrow night will be a perfect time to start a recon mission. The snow will give us great cover, help keep our steps quiet."

"You certainly have been thinking about a lot of things during the last twenty-four hours, Walt. That mind of yours tired yet?" Lamar chuckles at his own joke.

"Yes to both. My brain is in overdrive and exhausted. That's why I wanted us to all come clean about things. I've been fighting my own personal demons the last few days. The man I used to be tried to take over, and part of him does need to come out if we want to live. The other, darker side, needs to go away, because that part of me wants me to do whatever necessary to live, even if it's wrong."

"Yep, you fell and bumped your head." Lamar grins. "No doubts now."

Jesse's heart pounds inside her chest. Walter turns his attention back to her and walks over. She stiffens, ready for round two of the fight.

Instead of another dressing down, he puts an arm around her shoulder and smiles. "I'm sorry I put you through that, but you needed to let it out. You aren't the only one in our little group here with issues. We all have them. The trick is to lean on each other for support.

Can't have the woman my son loves anywhere but right by his side. Can't risk any of us falling by the wayside, either. We're all one big, messed up family now."

"Well, I'll be damned." Martha mutters from across the room. "I'll be damned."

From the corner of her eye, Jesse notices Kyle bend over and whisper into Turner's ear before passing him something. Turner smiles and tears glisten in his eyes. She is so stunned by Walt's words, never, ever dreaming she'd hear him say such things, all she can do is smile and hug him.

"Since we're coming clean about things, I've got something to add." Mike Bailey pipes up.

"And that is?" Walt pulls away from Jesse's embrace.

Mike rises. Jesse senses he is close to breaking down. "Things went downhill so fast on Saturday it was all kind of a blur. I didn't really have much time to think ahead. I mean, trying to grasp all the chaos was overwhelming. But, since I've had a chance to ponder things, I've decided to leave."

"Are you insane?" Lamar gapes at him.

"No, he's not. Neither am I." Deputy Allsop adds. "Like Bailey said, things were so intense Saturday, all we could think about was saving our asses, and putting as much distance between us and those hungry creatures from Hell. Now that we've had time to come down from the insane high, we've decided to head out."

"Why? Where?" Martha asks.

"I've got family in Bentonville, Ms. Martha. The last contact I had was the day before all this shit went down. I can't stay here without knowing what happened to them. It'll eat me alive."

"Bailey's right, Ms. Martha." Allsop nods. "Same thing with me, though my parents are in Branson. We planned on heading out together tomorrow. Walt? I know all about your tracking skills. If you want to go out tomorrow night, see if we can locate them government men, then I'm up to waiting another day before we leave. I owe you my life. You with me, Bailey?"

Shifting uncomfortably from one foot to the other, Bailey finally mutters, "Yeah, but only one day. Then, I'm going. No matter what."

"Bailey, did you say Bentonville's where your kin lives?" Lamar asks. Bailey nods. Lamar shifts his gaze over to Walter and smiles. "Bentonville. You thinking what I'm thinking?"

Walt returns the grin. "See there? Things sometimes work out perfect when thoughts ain't no longer hiding in the shadows of our minds. Yep, I sure am, Lamar. Couldn't have asked for a better segue into the next topic of discussion."

"Speaking of secrets, want to let the rest of us non-preppers in on this conversation?" Reed asks.

"I mentioned earlier we needed more supplies. I planned on asking for volunteers to make a trip to Bentonville, and now, it seems I have some."

Mike Bailey laughs. "Well, I'll be. You planned on raiding one of them temperature-controlled warehouses up there owned by Walmart, didn't ya?"

"Yes. So how about this as the plan? Me, Reed, and Kyle will accompany you both. We'll help you find out what happened to your families. If we find them, they can come back with us. If we don't, will you both come back with us? Hole up here? You know, after we grab us some grub and fill up some trucks?"

Bailey and Allsop exchange glances. Both nod in agreement.

"Good! Either of you know how to drive a semi?"

The room explodes with a million questions. Jesse steps away from Walt and walks back over to Turner. Bending down, she places a warm, gentle kiss on his forehead. "Sorry you had to hear all that, babe. Forgive me?"

Raising his uninjured arm, Turner reaches out, stroking her cheek. "Nothing to forgive. We've all got things we struggle with. You're the addict, I'm the klutz. What a pair, huh?"

Jesse chuckles softly. "Match made in Heaven, baby."

"Since everyone else ain't paying us no attention, I've got something to ask you. Been on my mind for quite a while so please don't think it's a spur of the moment, end-of-the-world kinda thing. I had it all planned out—a big surprise at Christmas. The plans and the location changed, but the feelings haven't."

Turner holds up a ring.

Jesse gasps.

"I've loved you from the moment we met, even when we were apart. Will you please do me the honor of saying yes?"

"Oh, Turner, it's beautiful." Jesse whispers through tears. "Yes, yes, of course I will."

Turner slides the ring on her trembling finger. "I know things are different now, and a wedding and such ain't in the cards, but it don't matter to me. Knowing we're together, even in this mess, is everything."

"I can't believe you didn't lose it, especially after that wicked fall. Talk about lucky!"

"That ring is more than lucky. It's special."

Jesse turns around at the sound of Kyle's voice. To her surprise, she notices tears in his eyes.

"I loved your mother, Jesse. So much. Planned on asking her the same question this past Sunday, but the world crapped out before I had the chance."

"Oh, my God." On instinct, she moves closer to Kyle and hugs him. Loud enough for only Kyle to hear, she says, "I knew it! I knew you two were an item. Jesus, Kyle, I'm so sorry."

"Me, too, Jesse. I miss her so much, but at least the love we shared will carry on..."

Kyle pulls away after choking up. Jesse watches him walk toward the alcove where the bathroom is, tears of her own running down her face. Once Kyle disappears, she stares at the ring. It is lovely and fits her finger perfectly. Even if it had been a piece of string, the emotional impact it represents wouldn't have changed.

I love you, Mom.

She returns to Turner's cot. "Your dad was right about secrets. Mom hid her own from me, and look what happened? I knew she was seeing Kyle, yet she never said a word. Maybe he'da asked her sooner if..."

"Don't, Jesse. The past can't be changed. We'll just learn from it and move forward. Together."

"I love you, Turner Addison. I promise I'll make you happy. I promise. Thank you for being my sunshine in this dark world."

Turner starts quietly humming "My Girl." Soon, the entire group of freaked out family and friends join in, gathering around Turner's cot. The humming switches to singing, and they all belt out the words.

Martha, Jane, and Jesse cry while in the middle of a group hug. When Uncle Reed leans down and embraces Turner, there isn't a dry eye in the room. For a few, blessed minutes, they forgot all about why they were trapped inside a cave.

Chapter 6 - The Road to Hell is Paved with Blood and Pain

Tuesday, December 23rd – 6:15 p.m. – Mountain
Standard Time

TERESA ALVARADO IS physically and emotionally spent. She hasn't eaten in two days and finished off the last dribbles of water four hours prior. Though she's tried numerous times, there was no way for her to extract herself from the rubble to search for more.

Trapped inside the demolished building, body surrounded by chunks of debris, she's lost feeling in her lower left leg after a heavy piece of ceiling landed on top of it. She lacks the strength to move it.

Tired, alone, and frightened beyond words, she can only listen for any odd noise outside. Other than an occasional gunshot or faint scream, everything is deathly quiet.

The silence is scary, yet not near as terrifying as the explosions. The only good thing she can find in the situation is the dead have yet to discover her location.

The roof is gone, leaving her exposed to the elements. She prays for rain, but so far, nothing. Looking into the sky, she notices the thick, grayish smoke still hanging heavy in the air. The orange and red rays from the setting sun are barely visible through the haze.

She wants to cry, yet is so dehydrated, no tears come. Phoenix is gone, and the fact she survived the blasts is still inconceivable. The place she'd hidden inside when the bombs rained from the sky allowed her body to survive, but what she found before the missiles destroyed the city, killed her soul.

The stillness opens her thoughts to the horrific trip she endured, alone, during the last three days.

And remind her why she's given up on living…

***

…Interstates 10 and 17 are so crammed with vehicles, some on fire, others full of shredded, rotting corpses, she turns around and heads toward the outskirts of Phoenix.

She needs more weapons to survive the nightmare and find Maria. The only place she knows for certain to find some—along with plenty of ammunition—is the old warehouse Roberto owns. The way she figures things, Roberto had probably been on his way there to load up, only to fail.

"Ha, I hope your body looks like Swiss cheese now! No, that would be too easy. I hope those monsters ripped you apart and you were alive long enough to watch them eat you!"

Nerves on edge and mind spinning from too much stimulation, she weaves her way through town, numb by shock and grief. Never, in all her life, has she seen such awful things. People run through the streets while being chased by the dead, and those who aren't fast enough, tripped, or simply couldn't run any longer, are torn apart in seconds.

Part of her wants to help, yet she knows she cannot. She isn't a warrior, and only has six bullets in the gun. To survive long enough to find her sister, she must turn a blind eye to the carnage all around her and stick with the original plan.

Watching people die horrible deaths as they fall victim to the monsters, knowing there isn't a thing she can do to help, makes her heart heavy with sorrow.

She spotted several military trucks along the way, panicking each time one came into view. Each time one appeared, she stopped the Navigator and crouched down in the seat, figuring if they passed by, they'd assume the SUV was yet another abandoned vehicle and keep going.

That plan worked fine the first three times while she inched her way toward the warehouse, but will it this time?

Stopping as a caravan speed out of town, she peeks out the driver's window, shocked to see the soldiers leave in such a hurry. She doesn't look out the passenger window until a loud, pounding noise on the glass catches her attention.

Spinning around, she panics. Two undead things claw at the window. Fumbling around for the gun in the seat, she bumps into the button controlling the passenger window. Screaming at the top of her voice, she tries to push the button in the opposite direction, but the corpses outside already have their bloody, gory arms inside.

"You won't stop me from finding my sister!" Her fingers finally latch around the gun's grip. "You won't! Go back to Hell!"

Four shots take out the unholy monstrosities and they disappear from the window. Deciding to take her chances with the military, she jumps back into the driver's seat, slams the gear into drive, and floors it.

The military vehicles don't seem to notice, so she keeps going, controlled by complete and total hysteria, driving over curbs, sidewalks, and dead bodies, not even registering the disgusting sounds as the corpses explode underneath the Navigator's tires. All she can think about is getting more weapons so she can head to the airport and search for Maria. The revolver only has two shots left, and she needs more to fight her way through the hordes of the dead.

It is difficult to make out her location since the streets are littered with vehicles and bodies. She pushes on, winding through the cluttered streets, tires barking when taking curves too fast.

Finally, she recognizes the road leading to the warehouse. Another group of military vehicles blows past her at a blinding pace. Ignoring them, she continues forward, stopping only inches from the front door.

Grabbing her bag and keys, she jumps out of the SUV. The terror from before ignites into an inferno of panic when a strange sound makes her look up.

Military planes streak across the bright, afternoon sky. Squinting, she notices missiles shoot from them, and realizes why the soldiers were racing to leave.

"Oh, my God! They're going to destroy the city!"

Bursting into a full sprint, she dashes into the building. It is old, made from solid concrete, and she prays it will offer shelter from the bombs.

She only makes it halfway inside when the ground shudders underneath her feet as the first bombs explode outside. Something to her left catches her attention. "No. No, it can't be! How? Why? Mi hermana bebé dulce!"

Dropping to her knees, she weeps over what is left of Maria. She's turned into one of the vile monsters. Someone shot a bullet into her head and sliced through her neck and breasts, too. A chunk of rancid flesh hangs from Maria's blue lips, another large piece of skin clamped between her stiff fingers.

Any doubts Teresa had the disgusting mess is her beloved baby sister vanish when she spots the engagement ring.

Turning away from the nightmare, unable to comprehend how Maria ended up on the warehouse's kill floor, Teresa vomits. While in the middle of puking, mind way past the point of sanity, the building explodes.

She welcomes the end, because the only reason she's kept going, is already dead...

***

…"God, please just take me. Now. Even Hell is better than this." Teresa whimpers. "I don't want to remember these things while I slowly starve to death!"

She hates passing out because the haunting images replay inside her mind. Being awake and remembering them isn't any easier, either. She's given up on surviving and prays for the sweet release of death, but God isn't listening, granting her requests to have a heart attack or simply for her blood to stop pumping.

"Please, God. Let me move enough to grab the gun. I'll gladly face your wrath for taking my own life rather than waiting for one of those monsters to come tear me apart. I don't want to die the way Maria did. Why? Why did you let this happen to us? To my sweet sister?"

Her pleas to God are interrupted when she hears a noise. Straining to listen, she realizes it is tires crunching through the debris. The noise stops, followed by doors opening and footsteps.

Forgetting all about her prayers to die, a spark of hope ignites inside her chest. "Help! Please, help me! I'm trapped."

The footsteps move faster toward her position. She offers a silent prayer, begging God to not let the men be soldiers.

"Prisa! La mujer sigue viva!"

Teresa's excitement at hearing Spanish makes her heart race. "Estoy por aqui. Por favor apurate!"

A man's face appears above her head. He scans the small space she is crammed inside. Her heart pounds from joy. "Miguel!"

"Teresa?"

"Yes! Oh please, help me. My leg is stuck. And water. I need water."

Miguel's face disappears, and the sounds of the others grow fainter. Someone tosses a bottle of water and an apple over the edge. She catches both, alternating between guzzling the cool liquid and tearing out huge chunks of the sweet fruit.

"Any broken bones?" Miguel yells from above.

"I don't think so. My leg's trapped, though. I can't lift the stuff on top of it. Pretty sure it's just a flesh wound. Hurry, Miguel! I can't stand being down here another second!"

"Sí, Teresa. Un momento."

Miguel and the others move far enough away so she cannot make out their words. For a few seconds, she fears they've given up and left, until a rope drops from above.

"Hang on, we're coming." Miguel smiles. "You sure you're okay? We don't have a doctor up here. Hospitals are gone."

"No, I'm fine. Really. Please, hurry!"

Less than four minutes later, she is freed from the concrete prison. Miguel and Juan help her to the vehicle, holding her between them. The soft leather of their SUV is a welcome sensation on her sore, tired body.

Tomas, Miguel's younger brother, climbs behind the wheel. He glances at her in the rearview mirror, a crazed, hungry look on his face. Looking down, she realizes her shirt is torn, exposing her right breast. Grabbing the edges, she shifts the material.

"Here, mamasita, eat." Miguel offers another apple.

"Thank you." Teresa snatched the fruit away. She is beyond ravenous. "I can't believe you all found me! I thought this was it for me."

"Not yet." Miguel's hand touches her thigh and squeezes. "It will be, however, if you resist."

"Oh, God, no!" Teresa screams. On instinct, she fights back, clawing and kicking against Miguel's body.

Something smashes into the side of her head. Her vision blurs. Blood pounds inside her ears. With the last ounce of strength she possesses, she whispers, "Dios, este es el final. La salvación estaba tan cerca."

***

Moving. Is she walking?

No, she is in a vehicle. The excitement of realizing she is alive, and free from the crumbled building that had been her tomb, makes her heart thump with joy. She feels cool leather against her back and legs. And pain. Shooting, burning pain radiates from her left leg. She knows it isn't broken, but the deep gash and bruising hurt like crazy. The rest of her body aches as though she's worked out for twenty-four hours straight.

If she feels movement and pain, she is alive. Her mind is cloudy, full of a mishmash of jumbled thoughts. The giddiness wanes because she cannot determine if she is dreaming or awake. Strange sounds, smells, and new pain flood her mind, confusing her already deteriorated mental state.

She realizes she isn't asleep when a cold, strong hand reaches underneath her shirt, grabbing her breast. Her body reacts instinctually, squirming to move away from the intrusion.

"Not now, fool! I can't listen to her scream again. Wait until we stop."

The hand disappears. Her body trembles.

"The screams are half the fun, Miguel. Makes it more intense. She's still alive, so guess we didn't do any major damage."

"You are a sick pendejo, Juan. Sick."

"I don't remember you being bothered by her wails when it was your turn, Miguel. Admit it—you enjoyed it."

Miguel laughs. "True, but I didn't have a headache then. I do now. Too many hours on the road."

"Miguel, your head hurts because you haven't had any *llello*. I told you we shouldn't have left it in the tunnels, but no, you insisted. You're not the only one having withdrawals!"

"My insistence brought you this far, didn't it? You're still alive, Juan. Had we all listened to your plan instead of mine, we'd be like the rest of them: *cadavers andantes*! How was I to know Roberto's stash was already gone?"

"Mother Mary! We're in a world now with no cops in sight, free to snort up until our noses fall off, and not one line around. Figures. I should have stayed in the tunnels. I could have snorted my way into the next world!"

"Stop complaining, Juan. We've got some food, water, gas, guns, and pussy. No coke now, yet when we make it to Dahlert, we'll head right to our stash. In the meantime, if we want to keep our playtoy around, at least until we make it closer to Oklahoma, we should probably give her some more water. And food."

"Good idea. The entertainment isn't any fun when she doesn't move. Tomas? Where are we?"

"About thirty miles on the other side of Santa Fe. We're lucky the roads are practically empty here in the mountains. Want me to stop? No one's around. Besides, I'm ready for my turn of that *panocha* before it gets too stinky."

"Or Miguel's big *pene* rips her in half!"

All three men burst out laughing. Teresa mentally cringes. Disturbing memories flood her mind. Intense pain in between her thighs replaces the burning in her leg.

Oh, God. I remember now. What they did to me after pulling me free. What they're going to continue to do. They aren't saviors—they're devils!

Opening her eyes, she is greeted by darkness. Panic wells up inside her chest at the realization her arms are bound. Something covers her face. Unable to see, she is forced to rely upon other senses. She's heard three distinct voices—Miguel, Juan, and Tomas. Is it just the three of them, or are there more who have yet to speak? She tries, but cannot remember, how many she'd seen back at the slaughterhouse.

Mind scrambling, Teresa wishes she had the gun.

That won't help. It only had two bullets left. Besides, I can't move! Screw you, God. I'm not talking to you or asking for any more help. I'll handle things on my own.

The will to survive rises deep from within her mind, tearing away and destroying the woman she had been, replacing her thoughts with those of a deadly killer—just as lethal as the undead. The instinct to continue breathing, make it another day, overrides the fear pulsing inside her chest. Like a shot of morphine coursing through her veins, it numbs the pain.

Teresa Alvarado knows how to handle a man's wants and needs. She'll let the scumbags abuse her body, waiting until that small window of ecstasy consumes them and then, she'll strike with mortal blows.

Or, at least, take their favorite pieces of flesh with her on to the next life.

The shift in her mindset, the return to a predator crouched and ready to strike, gives her a sense of peace. Keeping up the illusion she is still unconscious, she remains still.

She doesn't think about their location, or the fact Miguel mentioned they are on their way to Dahlert, Oklahoma, where he is originally from.

Or food.

Water.

Sleep.

The gun.

All her thoughts converge on just one moment, and exactly how she'll execute it.

Thanks, Roberto, for paying for such a nice, strong set of dental implants. They're about to come in quite handy.

***

Strong fingers dig into Teresa's exposed arms, yanking her from the backseat. With almost zen-like control, she never gives into the temptation to cry out, even when tossed onto the ground. The sting of rocks digging into her back and elbows doesn't faze her in the least.

She's already endured enough pain for two lifetimes.

"Hope we didn't wait too long. She's not moving."

"Ugh, she does stink."

"So do you, Tomas." Miguel laughs. "Look, there's a small creek down the hill. No telling how long it'll be before we find fresh water again. I say let's put it to good use. Help me carry her down there."

"You two go ahead. I'm going to check out that SUV over there." Juan points toward the far side of the parking area. "Might be some stuff inside we can use, Miguel."

"Fine, but I can't promise you she'll still be breathing when you come back."

"No matter. Her body will still be warm."

Tomas and Miguel hoist her from the ground. She doesn't offer any resistance. It takes less than two minutes for them to reach the creek. Teresa hears the rushing water and guesses they are only feet away.

"Let me untie her. If we just throw her in, she might drown."

"You sure? What if she wakes up and tries to fight back, Miguel?"

"Tomas, you really think this little piece of spoiled, rich flesh can hurt you? You're a wimp."

The men continue berating each other while one of them unbinds her arms. Teresa's head bounces against the ground after he yanks the blindfold away. She uses the opportunity to open one eye. Both men have guns strapped to their thighs.

"God, I've always wanted to fuck her sideways. Roberto was a lucky man, getting to bang her every night. Of course, back then, she was pretty."

"Given what we've seen recently, I'd say she's stunning." Miguel's laugh is evil. "You got her?"

"Yeah."

"Good. Think I'll make a deposit behind those rocks first. All this stress has knotted up my guts."

Teresa hears Miguel walk away as Tomas lifts her off the ground. "Time for a bath, you El Salvadorian whore."

The cold water makes her gasp as her head and body go under. Grateful for the liquid, she opens her mouth, taking several gulps before her body freaks and she chokes.

Tomas grabs a handful of hair and pulls her head above the surface. "Ah, you're awake now. Good. I'm ready to see if I can make you scream with this."

Tomas' other hand grabs his crotch. Teresa notices he is naked from the waist down. He yanks her from the water, tossing her down on the embankment only feet away. The last rays of the sun help her while scanning the area.

No signs of Miguel or Juan.

Perfect.

In just a few seconds, she sizes up her quarry. Tomas isn't much taller than she is, thin as a rail, and young. Maybe twenty-two, if she remembers correctly. She can tell from the look in his eyes, the way he stares at her body, Tomas doesn't have much experience with women.

"You wish to fuck me, Tomas? Make me scream?"

Tomas' dark eyes widen in shock. They quickly narrow down into small slits while licking his lips. "Glad that pretty mouth of yours still works, Teresa. Yeah, I'm gonna do you right. Make you forget all about Roberto. And the others."

Pulling off the damp sweatpants she spreads her legs, letting a hand slide down between them. "Oh, I've already forgotten about them, Tomas. You know, after what's happened? Knowing any second could be our last moments alive—it's an aphrodisiac, don't you agree? I, too, have had my eye on you for some time. You are quite handsome. Juan and Miguel are too old. I've always had a thing for younger flesh."

Tomas' excited gaze shifts to what Teresa's hand is doing between her thighs. Looking around once more, seeing they are still alone, she bucks her hips toward Tomas' small erection.

"Hell yeah. I'm gonna take all of you, mamacita. Every hole will feel me."

Moving her other hand slowly toward Tomas' head, she gives it a gentle push. "I'm all clean now, Tomas. Have a taste before the others get back. Roberto always said my *pupusa* tastes like sweet nectar. He loved to lick me dry while I sucked his *paloma*."

The temptation is too much for Tomas. Flipping positions, he buries his face in Teresa's crotch while simultaneously shoving his cock into her face. She forces herself not to gag at the rank smell.

"No games, mamasita, or I'll cut you in half."

"None at all, Tomas," Teresa purred, grabbing the erection with her hands. She gives it a gentle stroke. "That's it, um, yes. Your tongue is magic."

The tension in Tomas' muscles relax as he digs in, nipping, licking, and biting. She pushes past the pain and zeroes in on her plan.

In one swift motion, and with the speed of a cat, she clamps her thighs together, smothering Tomas' face. With all her strength, she squeezes both legs and twists, muffling Tomas' screams.

Opening her mouth, she shoves the nasty piece of flesh inside and bites down, teeth ripping through the flesh with surprising ease. The bitter taste of copper fills her mouth as blood seeps from her lips. Turning her head, she spits out the limp chunk of flesh onto the ground. Hot, sticky blood pours from the wound onto her face and neck. Tomas' body jerks and writhes in agony, fingers clawing at her legs.

Years of yoga and kick boxing made her body strong. Though Tomas fights back, she holds on with every fiber of her being until his struggles lessen.

In seconds, Tomas' convulsions cease. Just to make sure he is dead, she reaches for a sharp rock to the right, grabs it, relaxes her thighs, and rolls left. Tomas collapses onto the ground, blood soaking the dirt underneath him. He whimpers only once before she smashes the rock into his temple.

Again.

And again.

And again, until Tomas' head is unrecognizable.

She glances at his chest and can tell he isn't breathing, so she scrambles to her feet and spots Tomas' pants and belt resting in a crumpled pile about ten feet away.

And the belt containing the holster with the pistol.

She smiles after checking.

It is loaded.

Hallelujah!

"Tomas? You done? My turn."

The sound of Miguel's voice is close. She dashes behind a boulder.

Miguel appears from the tree line, stopping short when his gaze settles on Tomas' remains. On instinct, his hand reaches for the gun on his hip.

Two shots break the quiet afternoon, yet they aren't from Miguel's pistol.

Or Teresa's.

They came from the direction of the truck.

Miguel draws his gun, immediately crouching low, mumbling under his breath, cursing the powers above while backpedaling toward Teresa's hiding place. The distance between them is about twenty feet.

Then ten.

Then five.

When less than two feet away, she raises the gun, holding the position until Miguel's head is inches away. Extending her arm, she sticks the barrel against the base of his neck.

Before Miguel has a chance to register his mistake, she pulls the trigger.

"That's two down." She smiles at Miguel's destroyed head.

"Ma'am? You okay?"

Teresa spins around at the sound of an unfamiliar male voice, gun pointed in front of her. Two men stand at the top of the rise. Father and son, maybe, judging by their ages. Only the elder one on the right has a gun.

"If you don't want to end up like them, go. Leave me be."

"Ma'am, we mean you no harm. I swear. I just shot the other man. He was trying to rob us. You weren't with them willingly, were you?"

She shakes her head.

"Looks like you handled yourself quite well, ma'am. Quite well. I'm Cooper Hollingsworth and this here's Mason Hall. We're survivors, like you, just trying to get home."

"Yeah, well good for you. Again, leave. I don't need—or want—any help. As you can see, I can take care of myself."

"I thought the same thing but changed my mind after seeing dead people chasing live ones. There's safety in numbers."

Teresa stares at the kid then back over to the other man. Part of her wants to believe them, but the other, stronger part, fears them enough to sacrifice the potential safety they offer.

The men who raped and tortured her are dead, and she now has three weapons and a vehicle, but where will she go? Drive around until the gas runs out? There is no home to go back to; no one waiting to be rescued. The shakes set in.

"Please, ma'am. It'll be dark soon, and it's much harder to stand guard against the dead at night. We stopped here to refill our gas tanks, eat, and rest up a bit. Planned on leaving soon." The older man appears sincere. "You can stay in your vehicle with the doors locked. We'll do the same. Just, please, come on up here. Won't sit well with my soul if we just leave you all alone out here."

Teresa lowers the gun, steps over Miguel's body, grabs his weapon, and then moves over to where Tomas' pants sit in a crumpled heap. After yanking them on, she almost laughs at the absurdity of wearing the clothes of a man she killed.

She shoves the extra gun into the waistband before looking over her shoulder. The men haven't moved.

"I did this to both of them and won't hesitate to kill again if either one of you tries to hurt me. I swear."

"Don't doubt that one bit, Miss?" Cooper's tone is friendly and calm.

"Names don't mean shit anymore. Keep your distance. I'll be gone by morning."

Teresa makes her way up the hill, gun trained on the men named Cooper and Mason. They back away until she slips inside the SUV. When she locks the doors, both turn and head back toward their own vehicle.

Setting the guns in the passenger seat, she searches for food and water. A few backpacks crammed in the front floorboard sport plenty of supplies. She eats and drinks until she can do neither anymore while night descends from the sky.

For the next several hours, she keeps an eye on the vehicle with the two men, waiting, watching for any signs of movement. Though the one named Cooper mentioned they wouldn't hang around long, they had yet to leave. She concludes they are going to leave her alone, so she climbs over to the backseat and digs around to see what else is inside, happy when discovering her purse.

The trio of fools hadn't touched anything inside of it, including the money, and Roberto's journal. Digging deeper, she remembers her makeup bag contains a few items of use inside. Yanking it out, she feels around until finding the hand sanitizer and a few tampons. She cleans her hand before taking the cotton from the tampons and dabbing some sanitizer on them, and then sets about cleaning the wounds to her face, arms, legs, and chest.

All her other wounds will simply have to heal on their own. Some, she fears, will be with her permanently.

She pokes and digs around every inch of the SUV, looking for anything of use, stuffing a flashlight and extra batteries inside her bag, along with a long switchblade. A small squeal of delight fills the interior when she finds an entire carton of cigarettes from underneath the front passenger seat. Though she gave up smoking years ago, the craving rushes back while holding a pack in her hands.

If ever there is a time to smoke, it is now. A victory puff for the new woman she became.

She is, after all, the daughter of Mario Alvarado. Today, her actions made him proud. The memory of standing in the den at home, forcing her mind to imagine herself as a badass, is now her new reality.

Teresa cusses a blue streak upon realizing there isn't a lighter anywhere inside the SUV.

"Duh, use the one in the dashboard."

She turns the key in the ignition and pops the lighter. The first few drags make her cough, but she pushes on and keeps puffing. Soon, the interior fills with smoke, and she needs to pee. Grabbing a gun, she opens the door and steps out into the chilly night air.

Pausing, she scans the area for any signs of movement. Seeing none, and only hearing the faint sound of a vehicle or two on the main road, she holds the smoke between her lips and squats next to the back tire. Just as she yanks the pants back up, the sound of a vehicle approaching at a high rate of speed catches her attention.

Flinging the cigarette to the ground, she jumps back inside the SUV. Headlights bob and weave from a car careening down the road, heading straight toward her position. Starting the engine, she shoots forward.

Not fast enough.

The runaway car clips the back quarter panel. The impact forces her head into the steering wheel. On instinct, her foot stomps on the brake.

Dazed from smacking her head, she watches the accident unfold in front of her eyes.

The car rolls down the hill at full speed, only stopping after it smashes into a clump of trees. Smoke plumes from underneath the crumpled hood. Two bodies crash through the windshield, flying at least ten feet in the air until they land with a sickening crunch on the ground.

"Holy shit!" Teresa rubs her forehead. "That was close!"

Putting the SUV in park, she steps out to assess the damage, not even glancing back to see if the occupants of the car need aid. If either of them survived being ejected from the car, their injuries will be too much for her to do anything about anyway since she has no medical supplies, no training, and honestly, no interest in helping people who just damn near ended her life.

"Well, that's just fucking great! Hope there's another tire in the back." Teresa shakes her head upon seeing the flat tire. "Who am I kidding? I don't know how to change one, anyway."

The crunch of dirt behind her from footfalls causes her to spin around. Cooper and Mason are running toward the creek. The stupid men are going to see if they can help, and perhaps risk injuring themselves in the process. They'll be back once they realize the mission is pointless.

She makes up her mind to ask for assistance changing the tire and then get the hell out of the eerie mountains. If Cooper Hollingsworth and Mason Hall won't willingly help, she'll give them some incentive in the form of a gun pressed against the old man's head.

Stepping back to the driver's door, she leans in and grabs a gun.

Bam. Bam. Bam.

The three gunshots caused the hairs on her skin to stand erect. Looking up, she peers out the passenger window, but cannot make out much in the dark.

"I missed them!" Cooper screams. "Get back to the vehicle! Now!"

"What's going on?" Teresa yells.

"Zombies heading your way. Come on, follow us!" Mason bursts past the front of the SUV, Cooper right on his heels.

Teresa looks back toward the accident scene. Sure enough, two corpses are heading in her direction.

Fast.

Instincts kicked in, blocking her misgivings about Cooper and Mason. Snatching her purse and gun, she leaves the broken-down SUV and follows the two men to their own. Though she runs with everything she has, pushing her muscles to their limits, she senses the creatures are only steps away.

The trio make it to the SUV with mere seconds to spare. Just after shutting the door, the first corpse slams into the side, cracking the glass. The vehicle shudders.

"Hurry the fuck up! Go! Go! Go!" Mason screams.

Cooper cranks the engine to life and guns it. "Hang on!"

Watching with shock and disbelief as the second zombie launches itself into the air, landing on top of the roof, her mouth goes dry. The thing pounds on the glass of the sunroof, trying to break through.

"Do something, Cooper!" Mason yells.

Cooper responds by slamming on the brakes. The maneuver works, and the monster flies from the roof, tumbling over the hood to the ground. Teresa looks out the back window. Her stomach clenches as the other one grabs onto the back bumper.

"Fuck this." Teresa raises the gun.

"Wait!" Mason yells. "Don't shoot! There're gas cans in the back and we need that window in one piece."

"I won't get torn apart by that foul thing!"

Cooper tromps on the gas, throwing her off balance. She bounces around the back seat like a ragdoll as the vehicle does donuts.

"It's gone! Go!" Mason shouts.

The roar of the engine as they flee the rest area sounds like music to Teresa's ears. She resituates her body in the seat and looks behind them. The corpses try to keep up, but they are no match for the speed of the SUV.

"I had no idea they were so fast." Teresa swallows hard. "How can they move like that? Their bones are broken. The ones in Phoenix didn't move that quick. Then again, the ones I saw didn't just crash through a windshield, either."

"Welcome to Hell." Cooper sighs. "Anything's possible here."

For the next ten minutes, no one speaks. She stares out into the dark night, convinced she's finally gone insane. As the adrenaline rush wanes, the shakes set in.

She takes a deep breath. "Teresa."

"Why don't you get some rest, Teresa?" Cooper's southern accent is oddly comforting. "I'll need you to take over driving duties soon. That is, if you wish to continue with us. Like I said before, I promise we won't hurt you. We're heading back to my hometown in Arkansas. My kids are there."

"Are you two related?" Teresa asks.

Mason turns around in the seat. "No. Actually, we just met yesterday in Steamboat Springs. Cooper's a cop, or, well, he was. He's good people. He saved my life; tried to get me back to my family."

"Tried?"

"Santa Fe's gone. Along with Denver, Steamboat, and probably every other big town. Nothing remains but piles of smoldering rubble. Seems the government's response was to carpet bomb infected cities. Looked like people tried to flee, but they didn't make it. The roads were impassable. That's when I decided my best chances of surviving rested with him."

Teresa remains quiet as the words sink in. Whatever is going on isn't just contained in Arizona. "Phoenix is, too."

"Damn." Mason lowers his gaze.

"Bombed, you mean?" Cooper asks.

"Yes. I was trapped inside a building when those men found me."

"Ah, now I understand your apprehension. You thought they were helping you, but they turned out to be monsters of another kind. Right?"

"Yes, and I knew them. You and Mason are strangers."

"True, yet sometimes, strangers turn out to be blessings." Mason pats his chest. "I'm living proof. So, you mentioned you were trapped in a building?"

"Yes, I was. Roof collapsed on me when the bombs exploded."

Cooper glances at her in the rearview mirror. "There's a first aid kit back there somewhere if you need it. Also, there's a suitcase with some of my wife's clothes. Probably too big, but at least they aren't covered in blood, and didn't belong to monsters."

Hearing the hitch in Cooper's voice, she considers asking about his wife, but decides she really doesn't care why Mrs. Hollingsworth isn't around. Instead, she reaches behind her, feeling around for the suitcase. The thought of wearing Tomas' pants any longer makes her skin crawl.

"Any broken bones you need help with?" Mason asks.

"No, but I do have a deep gash that could probably use some antiseptic and a bandage." Teresa spots the white kit on the floorboard behind Cooper.

"Need some help?"

"No. Well, yes. Hold the flashlight for me, Mason?"

"Sure thing."

Teresa digs out the light from her bag and hands it to Mason. It takes several minutes, but she finally manages to clean and dress the wound.

"Thanks." Teresa holds her hand out for the flashlight. "Appreciate you both keeping your eyes on the road while I change."

Mason smiles before turning to face the front. "Now that you're patched up and in fresh clothes, like Cooper said, you should rest."

A prickle of worry slithers up her back as she tugs off the jeans. "Mason, why don't you just take over when Cooper tires?"

"Oh, I would, but there's one little problem."

"What's that?"

"I don't know how to drive."

Staring at the back of the kid's head, she wonders if he is lying. She doesn't get the vibe he is, so she continues putting on a warm pair of sweatpants and a thick sweater. "You're serious?"

He nods.

"Jesus, how old are you? Twelve?"

"Seventeen, thank you very much. I had strict parents. They bought me a car for Christmas, and I was going to take driving lessons after the first of the year."

Teresa shakes her head. Mason is just a young, spoiled rich kid, just like she'd been.

Both men seem frightened, perhaps because they'd been on the road quite some time, if they told the truth and their original starting point was in Colorado. They'd probably seen—and maybe participated in—a variety of disturbing events. Yet through all the horrors they'd surely endured, Teresa senses their kind spirits. After all, they did warn her when the monsters were coming, and no one else she knows—or knew—would have been so kind. They would have simply run away and let her be the bait.

The duo saved her life. She decides to trust them, at least for the time being until they prove her wrong.

"Okay, I'll drive when it's my turn, but I'm not tired. Too much is going on. I've got some reading to catch up on."

"Thanks, Teresa. Glad I'm not the only geek inside the vehicle. Hope you're reading something happy because every horror novel just became nonfiction. One more question, though? I want to see if I'm right."

"About what?"

"Your accent. El Salvador, correct?"

"How did you know?"

"My dad worked for a pharmaceutical company, and one of his co-workers was from San Salvador. They were working on a big deal to manufacture some kind of pill that helps with erectile dysfunction, and the meetings had to be in person. One of Dad's interns went to El Salvador with us. His name is Daryl Riverside."

"Is there a time when this story answers the lady's question?" Cooper chuckles.

"Sorry. My mom always said I should've been a writer because I like to set the scene. Anyway, one summer, about seven years ago, my family went on a trip to San Salvador for my dad's work. He was gone most of the time, but Mom and I had a blast. The beaches are stunning. Mom begged Dad to put in for a permanent transfer after the second day of the trip. Of course, all that changed after Daryl disappeared."

"Disappeared?" Cooper asks.

"Yeah. Thought my parents would have heart attacks before we got back to the states. Dad said the authorities concluded Daryl had been kidnapped by a drug cartel ring, run by some guy named Alvarez. No, that's not right. Alva...Alvarado. Yeah, that's it. Anyway, after that happened, my family high-tailed it back to the states. Before Daryl vanished, I loved the place. Your accent is beautiful, Teresa. I'm surprised I remember it so well."

Teresa's heart flutters inside her chest, overcome with gratitude she only gave her first name earlier.

Holy shit. Daddy's legacy, even in the middle of this nightmare, still lives on. I can't believe he knew Daryl Riverside. I remember him! Tall, lanky, ugly American. Daddy brought him to the estate once. Pft! Daryl certainly hadn't been kidnapped. He'd come willingly. Those two days he spent at the estate, holed up in secrets meetings with Daddy—oh, the irony. I'm in the middle of nowhere, on the run from walking corpses, and bump into someone with ties to my past. Unreal.

"Well, you were right. I'm originally from El Salvador. Now, do you mind, Mason?" Teresa holds up the journal.

"Oh, sorry. Sure thing."

Teresa blocks out the murmurings of the duo as they gab in the front seat. She trusts them, but not enough to fall asleep. Instead of resting, she grabs the flashlight and Roberto's journal from her purse and starts reading.

She hopes to find account numbers, passwords, or locations for all the money Roberto stashed around the world. Surely, whatever Hell is happening in the United States isn't occurring everywhere. Maybe she'll get lucky and find some in the Caymans or Bahamas. Going to Arkansas with the two men won't be such a bad idea, since it will put her closer to the ocean.

All the thoughts about money, finding a new home in a warm, tropical location similar to El Salvador, vanishes after reading the last two months' worth of entries.

Oh. My. God.

Roberto, Benito—you bastards!

Maria. My sweet, naïve, blind Maria. Now I know why you were at the slaughterhouse. He used you as a mule, and Roberto knew of the plan. I...oh, Jesus! I can't believe it. For days I wept, begging Benito and Roberto to do something to find you—and they knew all along.

Roberto Sanchez—I hope you aren't dead. I hope you are a walking cadaver, doomed to forever roam in search of food, yet never find any.

Maria. My sister. I knew I should have brought you with me to the states and away from that crazy San Salvadorian!

Benito San Nicholas—if you're alive, you better start praying. Ask the Virgin Mary to let the dead get to you before I do because I swear, I will do whatever it takes— kill whoever stands in my way—to get back to El Salvador and find you.

When I do, you'll beg me to end your suffering. I won't, though. I won't. I'll make sure you feel all the pain you caused my sister. And me.

All of it. The road to your personal Hell will be paved with blood and pain.

Lots and lots of excruciating pain. You took away my reason for living yet provided me with a new one. Revenge, Benito. My focus, my entire being, is now controlled by revenge.

Closing the journal, she stares out the window, any semblance to her old life completely obliterated from her thoughts.

LAMAR CROUCHES NEXT to Walter, studying the tracks covered with fresh snow. Shaun watches from several steps back, eyes scanning the white-coated forest. He is tired from trekking through the woods, his mind and body still adjusting to the events of the last four days. They'd taken an alternate route, opting not to attempt a journey down the slippery slope Turner fell from the day before. When they passed the glen with the graves, he felt sick to his stomach.

"That way." Lamar points west with the tip of his rifle.

"Agreed." Walter rises to his feet. He clicks off the flashlight before sticking it back inside his pocket.

Shaun scans the forest one last time before moving to join the rest of the men. Though it is late, the moon is bright. Silvery rays bounce off the fresh snow. "How can you be so sure? The snowfall covered most of the tracks, right?"

"Yes, the ones where they walked alone, but the ones made when they were carrying the body are deeper. See?" Lamar points to the right. "Thank God we only got a few inches of snow, or we'd be screwed."

"Okay, boys. You know the plan. We follow these tracks until they lead us to their location. Once they do, we'll know where the bastards are hiding. After that, we draw them out with this."

Shaun stares at the makeshift Molotov cocktail Walt rigged earlier. That part of the plan he didn't like. While they'd huddled in the cave earlier, going over every detail of the plan, he'd suggested one of them act as a decoy and run to the encampment and beg for help. He'd even offered to be the one to do it.

Walt disagreed, saying it was too risky, because they had no idea how many people they were dealing with. His plan was to detonate the bomb, hide in the shadows, and pick off one or two to hold as hostages. Then, they would have leverage to negotiate with in exchange for information.

Shaun hadn't said another word during the planning phase, and now, he certainly wished he would have stood firm. Knowing what they are about to do makes him feel weird. It is wrong. The cop in him doesn't like the idea at all. A heavy sense of unease slithers around inside his gut, unable to shake the sensation they are walking into a trap, and he doesn't like leaving the rest of the group behind.

Reed Newberry is a tough man, but he isn't a spring chicken. Neither are Martha or Jane, and Turner certainly isn't in the position to offer help should something happen while they are on this foolhardy quest. And Jesse? Well, Jesse is the last person Shaun would entrust with a life. She is too jittery; too unstable.

Too young.

Shaking the doubts aside, he follows Walt, Bailey, Allsop, Kyle, and Lamar up the slight incline. Being outside in the woods, his gaze automatically scans the terrain for deer. He almost laughs out loud, wondering how the others would react if he broke ranks and took down a doe or buck.

He yearns to turn back and forget about the whole thing. They don't need to know any more than what they already do because whatever is in the air, soil, or each other, is turning people into flesh-eating monsters, the easiest solution is just to remain in the vicinity of the cave and stay away from the rest of humanity, only leaving when supplies need to be refilled. Maybe find a feed and seed store as they approach spring; plant a few seeds, slay some deer, maybe catch a few rabbits, breed them, and keep a constant supply of fresh meat handy.

He could do it. They all could. Learn to live off the land, naturally, the way God originally intended. There are plenty of beneficial plants to eat in the Ozark mountains to help sustain them. His memory is damn good, and he recalls reading several books written by a local author named Madison Woods. Marian had bought one of her books and given a signed copy to him as a Christmas gift the year prior.

Shaun smiles at the memory. Marian told him she worried about him spending so much time in the woods, fearing what would happen if he ever got lost or injured, so she purchased the book to teach him all he needed to know to survive out in nature should the need arise. That was one of the last, kind moments he'd spent with Marian, that Christmas morning the year prior. Weeks later, their marriage came apart at the seams.

The author wrote about how to spot wild ginseng and all its medicinal properties, along with other wild fauna and flora found in the mountains.

They could do it—they could survive, maybe even thrive—without exposing themselves to others and without killing individuals trying to do the same thing.

Shaking his head, he stifles a laugh. He is such a hypocrite. He didn't bat an eye when shooting the rocket launcher and killing the soldiers back in Malvern. He never gave it a second thought, but that was in the heat of battle, and the soldiers' intentions were obvious. No doubts. This time, though, is different.

They'd had time to regroup, think, breathe. What if the people they are stalking aren't part of the government? What if they're just like their small group—survivors who snagged military equipment and fled? What if they are other preppers? That would explain the bio suits. Maybe they were just burying a friend, taking extra precautions while doing so?

He nixes the ideas. They don't add up, either. Walt said one flipped his lid about fungus. Plus, Shaun already met Kevin Warton. He is in the military or maybe as he mentioned, ex-military. Walt and Lamar are both ex-Army, too.

Biting his lip, he shakes his head. He is going to drive himself insane thinking about all this. Then again, it is better than thinking about Marian or April or what is left of his wife and child in the aisleway of Malvern Walmart. How everything changed in the blink of an eye. God, no wonder his thoughts bounce wildly from one scenario to another.

He hates himself for thinking it, but he is glad his parents passed on before the world ended. He understands why Bailey and Allsop want to leave. He'd go insane with worry if any of his loved ones were still alive—and alone—trying to survive.

One minute, I'm out in the woods, enjoying myself, and the next—bam! Smack dab in the middle of Hell. A week ago, my only concern was about being a dad, and how I'd handle staying married to a woman who'd cheated on me. How I'd pay the bills with a new baby on the way. Wondering if I should get another job, since my ticker isn't as strong as it used to be. Or, maybe stay on the force, keep my heart issues quiet, and just get an additional part-time job to help with all the new expenses. Trading in my truck for a van to hold a baby seat.

Memories bombard him, swirling and churning inside his mind, but he freezes in his tracks when new, recent ones burst forward.

Craig's cocaine addiction.

Kevin Warton's reaction to the powder inside the bag, and his final words to Jesse. "Don't do drugs."

How fast people turned.

How fast the dead moved.

Jesus H. Christ. It makes perfect sense. Why didn't I make the connection before?

His internal musings cease when the others ahead of him stop. Walter points at the ground.

The tracks are gone.

"Walter? Wait, I think I figured out—"

"Be quiet!" Lamar hisses.

Walter creeps forward. All the man's attention is focused on studying the rock formation. Everyone except Shaun moves closer.

No. I'm going to say something. This isn't right! We shouldn't be here. Speak up, fool! You aren't afraid of an old prepper, are you? Besides, Walter said we should voice our opinions.

Just as Shaun opens his mouth to speak, his senses warn him something is wrong.

Not in enough time.

Cold steel presses against the back of his exposed neck.

"Drop your weapons, now, or I'll drop your friend."

No one moves.

"I said drop them!"

Shaun recognizes the voice. It belongs to Kevin Warton. "Easy, Mr. Warton. We were just—"

"Shut up!"

Another man appears seemingly from nowhere, right behind Bailey, sticking the tip of his rifle at the base of Mike's neck. Rather than hold still, Mike raises his weapon.

The sounds of crunching snow from numerous footsteps burst all around them. Kyle yells, "Shit! Munchers!"

Everything happens so fast; Shaun doesn't have time to register it all.

Shots ring throughout the quiet woods. His body falls backward, landing on top of Kevin. Rolling left, he tries scrambling to his feet, but the slippery snow makes the task difficult. Finally gaining some traction, he rises and pulls his gun.

More screaming; more gunfire. Burning pain explodes in the back of his neck, followed by searing heat throughout his chest. He gasps once before collapsing.

"Enough! Enough! It's over! We got 'em all. Fuck! He took two hits—a bite and a bullet!" Shaun hears Lamar yell from his right, but his voice sounds odd.

"Jesus, Joseph, and Mary!" Walter shouts.

"Oh, God! I tried to shoot through him to kill it!" Bailey sounds upset. "I aimed for the shoulder, Shaun, I swear. I'm so sorry!"

Footsteps converge on his position. Someone's hands press down hard on his chest. He tries make out who it is, but his vision is too blurry. Everything looks gray and fuzzy, like staring at the static on a TV.

"Son-of-a-bitch! Look at the size of that bite—"

"Never you mind, Lamar. Shaun? Shaun? Can you hear me? It's Walt."

"We've got a doctor. Here, help us get him up."

"Hear that, Shaun? You're fine, just stay calm, okay? These men have access to a doctor. Just hang on, son."

Walter's voice is faint. Shaun isn't sure he spoke, or he just imagined he did.

There is no more pain, no cold, damp ground soaking through the jacket. A weird buzzing inside his head drowns out everything.

Peace. There is warm, blessed peace up ahead.

"Come unto me, I'll give you rest."

The voice envelopes his mind and body, pulling him toward the warm, inviting light.

"Daddy. Come home."

"April?"

"Shhh, rest now. We're gonna take you to see a doc. Hang on, Shaun." Walter urges from somewhere distant, far away. "Hang on!"

"Don't listen to him, Daddy. Come home. Mommie and I are waiting."

"I'm coming, April. I'm coming."

***

Everett looks at the disheveled men standing around the makeshift operating table and with a heavy heart, shakes his head. "I'm sorry, but your friend will be gone in seconds. I tried, but the bullet did too much damage. He will turn not long after taking his last breath. The brain must be destroyed to prevent that. Now."

The room erupts with accusations hurled from both sides. He has never witnessed so many angry men confined into such a small area before.

"That's quite enough!" Dirk stands in between Warton and the man named Walter. "He's gone, and I'm sorry for your loss. Let's not add another to the body count tonight. We need to put him down before he reanimates. Please, step out into the hallway and I'll—"

"No. It's my fault. All my fault. Jesus, I've known Shaun since kindergarten. I'll do it."

"Bailey, right?" Dirk asks.

"Yeah. Mike Bailey."

Tension hangs thick in the air. Everett's skin prickles from the vast amount of energy confined into the meeting room. Yet another soul will pass inside the space.

He wants to find some comfort that the death of this man isn't on his shoulders, but that is impossible. All the twists and turns from this nightmare converge on his doorstep. Unwilling to look at the man's face any longer, he steps away as the distraught Mike Bailey takes his place.

The man is young, maybe thirty, tops. Everett says a silent prayer for his family—if he has any still alive.

"Bailey, you sure? I'll do it if you can't."

"No, Walt. Ain't gonna have the blood that belongs on my hands stain yours. Please, all of you, leave. I need to say my final goodbyes before I do it."

Everett winces when Bailey pulls a knife from his jacket. Tears slide down the man's cheeks, making some of his own appear. The rest of them leave the room in silence.

Once out in the hallway, Dirk addresses the new group of visitors. "What's happened can't be changed. It's over. Please, let's all take a deep breath and calm down."

"Calm down? We just lost one of our friends because—"

"Because we're all walking tight ropes and weren't concentrating on our *real* enemies. You know, the walking sacks of puss and goop out there?"

"Bullshit. Your men ambushed us *before* the dead made an appearance. How do we know you didn't use them as weapons against us?"

Dirk's face blanches. "Walter Addison, correct?"

A slight nod of the man's head is the answer. Everett senses the edginess from Mr. Addison and the others. Being around so many high-strung people, all with guns, makes his skin crawl.

"Don't take this the wrong way, Mr. Addison, but are you out of your fucking mind? Zombies as some sort of biological weapons? Jesus, how much TV did you watch before all this happened? Yeah, we sent the dead out to do our dirty work while watching how it played out, up close and personal. Think. Had that been our plan, we wouldn't have risked our lives, announced our presence, or worked on keeping your friend alive."

"He's right, Walt. That man there saved your life by shooting the one sneaking up behind you."

"Whose side are you on, Kyle?" Walter hisses.

"I'm on the side of living. Whether these men are soldiers or not, they tried to help. That one there—"

"Clive. Clive Winters. I'd say it's nice to meet you, but that'd be a lie."

"Okay, Clive Winters. He saved your ass from ending up like Shaun. In this insane world, that means everything. To me, at least. On behalf of our little group, I'd like to say thanks to all of you. We all could have died out there. Or worse."

"You're welcome, Kyle. As I mentioned before, this is not a government installation, and we aren't soldiers." Dirk takes a deep breath. "All of us are ex-military, except Dr. Berning here. We take orders from no one. The only reason the men were topside is because our sensors picked up movement outside. Unfortunately, the equipment only picked up your thermal signals since the others in the forest no longer generate heat."

"If you ain't working for ol' Uncle Sam, then what in the hell is this place? Why all the secrecy? The bio suits? Holding us at gunpoint?"

Everett realizes if any headway is to be made, it won't happen unless he steps in. After all, he is a civilian, too, and certainly looks the part. He hopes they'll believe him; realize an old man poses no threat.

Stepping forward, he pushes his fears away. Clearing his throat, he looked directly into the eyes of Walter Addison, who he senses is the leader. "Stop. Just, stop it. Who we are, or used to be, doesn't really matter at this point, does it?"

"Yeah, it sorta does." Walter's features harden. "After what happened to us before we made it up here, our trust meter broke."

"Fair enough, Mr. Addison. Allow me to formally introduce myself. I'm Dr. Everett Berning. Born and raised in Little Rock, attended college and taught microbiology and chemistry for years in Georgia. That is, until my entire family, all seven of them, died. A wonderful man named Dr. Jason Thomas—who, like me, also lost his entire family—brought me here to work on a project. A project fully paid for and put together by him and no one else. These men were hired by Dr. Thomas, each chosen for a particular skillset. Yes, they are all former members of the military, but the key word is *former*. They work for no one, including me. In fact, they are only here to help me with my research, which has now morphed over to finding some sort of cure for this unholy plague."

"You're...you're working on a cure?" Walter stutters.

"Yes. Well, I'm in the first stages of my research, but that is the goal. Now, recall Mr. Addison, it was you and your group attempting to remain concealed in the woods while searching for us, not the other way around. Am I wrong?"

Mike Bailey steps out from the room. The look on his face, the blood-stained hands, are enough proof needed to know he ended the life of his friend.

"Please, come this way, Mr. Bailey. We need to get that blood off you quickly." Everett whispers. "Dirk? Is it okay if we take them into the cafeteria and give them the answers to what I assume they were searching for? That was your goal—to find out what we knew—right, Mr. Addison? To gain as much information as possible; give you a leg up in a hostile world?"

Walter rakes a dirty hand across his face. "Yep, that was the plan. A poorly executed one, I might add. We didn't know—hadn't seen any evidence—the munchers were up here already."

"Deadly surprises are around every corner nowadays." Dirk points to the hallway. "This way, please."

***

An hour later, Everett's voice barely above a whisper from talking the entire time, the room is finally silent. He made sure not to mention anything about *Rememdium*, Daryl's betrayal or the botched rescue in Laredo, sticking only to what he's learned since the outbreak. A few times, he worried Kevin or one of the others would interrupt him and spill his shameful secret, yet they never did.

None of the men asked a question during the entire horrific presentation. It was the first time in his life he had completely commanded the attention of others. In stunned silence, they listened, hanging on to his every word. Occasionally, one gasped or cursed under his breath, but nothing more.

A few times he considered broaching the subject of the other danger posed by Arkansas Nuclear One in Russellville. Dirk, and the others, had not taken the news well when he broke it upon their return from burying Porterfield. After the load of shit he'd just handed out to the men, he couldn't get the words to leave his tired throat.

"Guess we know why you lost it when you thought Jesse took the drugs." Walt whispers.

Kevin rises and stretches before walking over to fix more coffee. "Yeah, I was kinda edgy that morning. Hadn't been that long since ol' Doc here dropped the good news into my ears. Plus, only a few hours since I had to put down my best friend. Wasn't anything personal against her, I can assure you. Is Jesse your daughter?"

Walt laughs, yet it sounds more like a cackle. "No. Not sure what to call her, exactly."

"That's cryptic, and rather creepy."

Walt shoots an irritated glance at Dirk. "Jesse and my son are an item. He, uh, just proposed to her yesterday. Back in the normal world, I suppose I'd call her my son's fiancé because they'd be planning a wedding. Considering the way things are now I don't think there'll be one. Ain't no one to perform the service anyhow. Or care, for that matter. I've never been too fond of the girl. She's a former drug addict, which in my book, especially in light with what you just shared, makes her a big liability."

"Interesting. Quite the dilemma for you as a father, and as a survivor."

"Bet when you go back and share all this happy news with your group, the girl will no longer be interested in drugs." Kevin snorts at his inappropriate joke.

"Since we've been so forthcoming with information, I think it's your turn, Mr. Addison." Dirk's features are expressionless, like a statue. "How did you even know we were here?"

Kyle chuckles. "Walt's son took a nasty tumble down the mountainside, right close to your graveyard. We saw ya'll. Kinda freaked when we noticed the bio suits. And the weapons. Graves."

"Ah, the assumption was made we were military, burying our secrets." Dirk's features relax. "I understand your concerns about us now."

Kyle shrugs his shoulders. "Live and learn, right? Okay, so, next question. Dr. Berning, you're sure this disease ain't airborne? We can only get sick if one of those munchers gets a bite in or we happen to find a stash of coke and snort it up?"

"Yes, Mr. Pender. I'm quite sure. The samples I've tested showed no signs of fungal spores in the lungs which means airborne transmission isn't possible. The fungi converge inside the brain."

"Which is why the only way to stop them is take out the brain. Makes sense." Walt shakes his head. "I just, good Lord. I can't wrap my mind around all this mess. Bodies controlled by fungus that crave human flesh. Un-fucking-believable."

"Yeah, you can't even begin to imagine how surprised the doc was when he figured it out. Choked him up." Kevin mutters.

Everett stiffens.

Dirk notices and rises. "Warton? I'll need some help securing Mr. Kilpatrick's remains in a bag. I'm sure these gentlemen are ready to head back to their camp."

Kevin settles his gaze on him, and the eerie smile on his face makes Everett's skin crawl. "According to the doc, we're supposed to incinerate any tainted remains. Remember?"

"Warton—hallway. Now."

Kevin and Dirk storm out of the room, leaving Everett standing in the middle with five sets of concerned faces staring at him.

"What's up his ass, Doc?" Kyle asks.

"I'm afraid Mr. Warton hasn't been the same since all this happened."

"Yeah, well, none of us have." Walter wipes beads of sweat from his furrowed brow. "And the thought of having to play mortician and burn a body doesn't make things any better, either. You sure that's the only way, Dr. Berning?"

"Quite."

"Then why did you let them bury Porterfield?"

"I've had a lot on my mind since all this happened, Mr. Addison." Everett blushes. "By the time I realized what they were doing, I was too late to stop them."

"If it's such a big deal, do you plan on digging him back up and disposing of him properly?"

"That's been discussed, yes."

"And the verdict?" Walter cocks his head.

"Due to the cold temperature outside, and the fact he's encased in thick plastic, we decided to wait."

"Well, I certainly don't want to do the same. The thought of digging Shaun up later makes no sense to me. Like you said, it's cold outside, and there ain't no leaves or dry brush to catch fire. We'll handle him once, then be done with it."

"A wise decision, Mr. Addison."

The men rise and gather their items. Walt pauses at the door. "We need to head back to our group. They're probably worried, since we've been gone longer than we anticipated. Just two final questions, then we'll take our friend's body outside and burn it."

"I'll answer them to the best of my abilities." Everett wishes his mouth wasn't so dry.

"No, these questions are for them." Walt motioned toward Winters, Rice, and Denton. "Y'all have any idea where those things came from? We ain't seen hide nor hair of one since we arrived. Hard to tell since they seemed burned and everything happened so quick, but I swear, it looked like they were wearing flight suits."

Everett's heart flitters. *The pilots! Oh, my God. We should have gone back!*

Clive Winters nods. "Yeah, it did to us, too. My guess would be they came from the wreck. When humping the trail up here on Saturday, a jet crashed about three klicks south. We were lucky it had already deployed the missiles, or we'd all be dead. Porterfield— the one you saw us burying—he and Warton searched the wreckage on Sunday. They didn't find any bodies, only the metal box with the blow inside. That's how Porterfield ended up turning. He snorted some. So, it seems, did one of the pilots."

"God, turned into a zombie from tainted coke. Unreal." Allsop's face is pale and sallow. "Do you think there's more out there?"

"Don't know." Clive shrugs his shoulders. "My guess would be no. Kevin said there wasn't much left at the wreckage site except the tail. He guessed it was an F-15, and that's a two-seater. Unless those flyboys came across others who fled to the hills, we're good. For now."

"What a nightmare." Bailey whispers.

"You mentioned questions. Was there another?" Denaryl asks.

Walt turns and looks at his men. Everett senses something unspoken passed between them.

"No, you answered both. We'll be on our way. Appreciate the intel. Good luck with your research, Dr. Berning. You pull it off and you'll be the new savi—"

"Please don't say it, Mr. Addison." Everett holds up a hand. "I've heard it before, and believe me, the title is a misnomer. Before you leave, I've got a question of my own."

"Shoot"

"You seem the type who was prepared for this, so I'm guessing your camp isn't exposed to the elements. Perhaps you've taken shelter in a cave, like us? Am I right?"

Walt's eyes narrow into small slits while studying his face. "Why do you ask?"

"Please, Mr. Addison, stop looking at me like I'm plotting something sinister. Since all this happened, we haven't come across other survivors, and it's nice to finally meet some. Knowing others have made it this far gives us all a ray of hope humanity will continue. Now that we've come across corpses up here, I just wanted to make sure you and the others are in a safe place. If not, I intended to offer sanctuary here. Nothing can penetrate these walls."

"Mighty neighborly of you, Dr. Berning. We'll certainly take it under consideration, should we have to leave our current location."

With that, the group leaves, including Denton and the others. Only Everett and Denaryl remain.

Denaryl huffs. "They're in a cave. Guaranteed. Sure doesn't look like they've been hanging their hats in a tent. Don't worry, Doc. They'll be safe, if what you think might happen in Russellville, comes to fruition."

Everett nods as Denaryl steps into the hallway.

"I don't think, I know." Everett whispers to the empty room. "Soon. None of us will be safe much longer."

Chapter 8 - The Journey

Wednesday, December 24th – 8:15 a.m. – Central
Standard Time

"REED, PROMISE ME YOU'LL be careful. No heroics. I need you to come back in one piece. So does Jesse."

"Promise."

Jane hugs his neck. "I know the trip is necessary, but—"

"Yes, it is. Especially since Bailey and Allsop might not return with us. While we've got the extra hands, we need to grab what we can. Losing Shaun last night wasn't only an emotional blow, it affected our safety, too."

"I still can't believe Shaun's dead. Thank God he didn't turn into one of those things and bite anyone else. Poor Bailey. He hasn't said a word since. He must feel awful. Tried to help his friend, and only ended up killing him. Twice."

"Yeah, he looks rough. I think he's already crossed the bridge over to Insanity Town. His mistake cost us all."

"Bullshit. Put the blame where it belongs—which is directly on the shoulders of those who started this mess. Any of us might find ourselves in a similar situation and make the same mistake. Firing a gun and hitting a target ain't easy, especially in the heat of things."

"For someone who's never been in combat, you're rather perceptive."

"My daddy taught me how to shoot when I was little, remember? I did just fine when there weren't any distractions. Hit the target every time. But, when he started making noises, jumping around, screaming, yelling, well, I couldn't hit the side of a barn."

"Yeah, real life certainly ain't portrayed correctly in movies. People panic, miss, and make stupid choices."

"If it comes to that for me, Reed Newberry, you know, if I get bit or something, you better put me down. I don't want to be—"

"Don't talk like that, Jane. Don't."

"Like Walt said the other day, it's harsh reality. I mean it, Reed. The thought of being one of those monsters, well, it ain't how I want to go out. Promise me, right now, you'll do it."

"Of course." Reed sighs. "Same goes for me."

Jane lets out a long breath. "It's Christmas Eve day. We should count our blessings Jesse didn't slip the other day, or she'd be a monster now, too."

"I know, and I'm grateful. You two are the only things keeping me from eating my gun."

"Reed!"

"Sorry, that was an internal thought that slipped out." Reed winks before pulling her closer, kissing the top of her head. "What little filter I had is long gone."

"You never had a filter. That's one of the many things I've always loved about you. You just let your thoughts fly."

Pulling away, she watches as he returns to the cot and laces up his boots. "You just said you loved me, Jane Richmond. Two words that haven't crossed those lovely lips since high school. Thanks for waiting to say it until we're inside a place with no privacy. I would have preferred hearing them when you are naked underneath me."

"Hey, at least I said them, right?"

"True. I love you, too, Janie-girl. Never stopped. Timing. Life's all about timing. My clock's always been off. I should've come back home sooner. If I had, we'd be hitched right now."

"Was that your weird way of proposing to me, Reed Newberry?" Jane smiles. "If so, talk about hearing things at the wrong time!"

"Hey, love is in the air, courtesy of Turner and Jesse. Guess it rubbed off. When any minute might be your last, you say what's on your mind."

"How romantic, Reed. I'm swooning over here." Jane glances around the cave, holding in a sigh of disgust. "Being married wouldn't change our current situation, anyway. We'd still be living in a freaking cave, hiding from walking corpses. God, that just doesn't sound right, does it? Hiding out from the dead."

"Jesus, it figures all this shit was caused from drugs." Reed's tone is full of bitterness. "They've been a plague of their own for years. Ruined so many lives, and special moments, like right now. I can't count how many times we busted people at the border. We barely scratched the surface—missed most of the shipments. Drug cartels were always finding new ways to sneak shit across. Guess the only good thing about this mess is the war on drugs is over."

Jane studies the face of the man she's loved since sixth grade. Reed's hair is thinner and white instead of dark mahogany. Age spots dot his forehead, nose, and hands. The skin on his face is deeply embedded with wrinkles from working outside for many years. She doesn't care. Not one bit. Reed Newberry has always been the kind of man who could have made his living in front of the camera. Rugged. Strong. Lithe and full of swagger. Clint Eastwood's body meshed with Sam Elliot's looks. The first time she saw him at the playground, she was hooked.

Other than his physical appearance, Reed hasn't changed much since high school. He is still the same brash, cocky man he's always been. A typical southern boy who loved his country, his family, and doing what's right, no matter who disagrees with his stances.

When she heard he was back in town, she felt like a giddy eighteen-year-old again. The rush to see him after nearly thirty years was overshadowed by the guilt she'd buried deep inside her soul.

Instead of exposing either of them to more heartache, she steered clear of him. A few times, she spotted his truck in the hospital parking lot when her shift ended, quietly sitting a few rows from her vehicle. Their high school romance had been ripped apart after she informed him she didn't want to continue their relationship while she attended nursing school.

Her harsh, cold words broke Reed's heart. Recalling the shocked look on his face still hurt. The wounded look haunted her dreams for years, even after marrying Russell Cotton, a doctor at St. Vincent's Hospital in Little Rock.

Fifteen years of marriage spent next to a man she thought she knew—a stable one with similar interests and ideals—ended after Russell left her for another woman. She'd been sad yet not heartbroken. After the divorce was final, she left Little Rock and moved back home to Malvern. In the back of her mind, she secretly craved for Reed to still be there, pining over her after years of being apart, only to discover he'd left and moved to Texas right after their high school graduation.

On instinct, her hand brushes across her flat stomach. Her uterus only housed a child once, and only for a very short time. The child conceived with Reed in their senior year only survived to the end of the first trimester. Jane was young, scared, and didn't want to become a parent at eighteen like her mother, so she went to Little Rock and had an abortion before breaking up with Reed a few days later.

The abortion wasn't done properly, and the procedure damaged her reproductive tract. Though she and Russell tried numerous times and spent thousands of dollars on specialists to help, she'd never been able to get pregnant again. During every visit to the doctor's office, every penny spent to treat her infertility, she kept the real reason for her inability to conceive from Russell.

The only person she'd ever told the shameful secret to was her mother, Ethel, years later after yet another unsuccessful round of medical procedures. Her mother's response cut Jane to the core: "God's punishment is upon you. You murdered a child and lied to the father."

The painful words spoken from the lips of her judgmental mother kept Jane from reconnecting with Reed when he moved back to Rockport. Thankfully, he never gave up pursuing her, and after months of trying, she couldn't fight the temptation to be with him again. They'd been seeing each other for several months before the world collapsed.

While staring at him, wondering if she'd ever see him again once he left on the supply run, she contemplated telling him the truth about the baby and that she never stopped loving him and thought about him for years. Explain he'd done nothing wrong in the relationship, like he'd assumed, and the breakup was her fault, not his. Apologize for hurting him, leaving such a wound to his heart he never trusted or loved another for the rest of his life. Tell him how her actions had stolen a chance for him to love again all because of a decision made on the spur of the moment.

The words perch on the tip of her tongue, but she can't say them. There is no reason to fill his head with painful truths of the past. Reed doesn't need extra mental baggage to carry around, not while exposed to the horrors he'd encounter on a trip to help their small group survive.

The secret will die with her, no matter what.

Shaking the past from her mind, Jane returns to the conversation. "I saw a lot of the side effects at the hospital, too. Accidents caused by people who were high; overdoses; domestic violence when one or both parties were wasted. Worked a few rotations in the neonatal unit, until my heart couldn't stand looking at another baby born addicted to whatever shit their mother used. Poor things stood no shot at living a normal life. And that was back before this started. In a weird way, it almost seems like this was the natural progression of things."

"Now you're starting to sound like Walt." Reed chuckles. "You usually ain't so cynical."

"Times change, Reed." She turns her gaze toward Jesse. "She hasn't said much since Walter dropped the news."

"No one has. Can you blame them?"

"Not at all. We've all got so much information to take in, plus mourn the loss of Shaun. We all thought we were safe here. Knowing some of those monsters were lurking about, so close to our location, smacked us back to reality. To find out we were wrong, well, it scared us all. Especially since ya'll are leaving."

"I know, babe. I know. Hopefully, the two were from the jet crash, like the other group said. Plus, that doc is working on a cure. Maybe he'll come up with something soon. At least we know this shit ain't airborne. That's another blessing."

Chills race up her spine. "I don't want you to go. I'm scared, Reed. Leaving us here, with only Lamar Wilson as protection? We're sitting ducks."

Boots on, Reed stands and clasps her hands in his. "We've already gone over this a hundred times, Jane. Lamar's survival skills, knowledge of the area, how to track, will serve the group better here. Besides, I'm a better shot than he is, and I know how to drive a semi. Lamar doesn't."

"My head gets that, but my heart doesn't. I can't lose you again. I can't."

Reed lets go of her hands, cupping her face with his strong fingers. "You won't. Promise. We'll be back in two shakes."

"That's a load of—"

Reed's lips crush the words of protest. She clings to him, drinking in every bit of his essence, imprinting his smell and taste. For a few electrifying seconds, she pushes all the worry from her mind and lets the rush of emotions take over.

The sound of someone clearing their throat ends the magical moment. Reed pulls away, his eyes full of love and passion, before turning his gaze to the voice behind them.

"Sorry to interrupt your little lovefest, but it's time to head out."

"Let me go say goodbye to Jesse first, Walt. I'll meet ya'll topside."

"We leave in five, so make it quick. Have you seen Kyle?"

"He went out about twenty minutes ago to check on Shaun's remains. Wanted to make sure they're gone, and that the fire's out."

"Oh, okay. Don't forget to grab some extra rounds before you head up."

"Walt, can't this wait?" Jane hates the fact her tone sounds like a pleading child. "There's snow on the ground so the roads will be dangerous."

"In a perfect world, yes. In this one? No. Bailey and Allsop are leaving today, and we need their eyes and ears to make this run successful. I'm sorry, Jane."

"I know." Tears fill her eyes. "I'm just worried."

"Then you have plenty to talk about with my wife." Walt pats her shoulder. "Already had the same discussion with her earlier. I'm sure our ears will be burning the entire time. Thank God divorce isn't an option anymore, or I'm afraid I'd be single."

Walt and Reed both leave Jane standing in the middle of the room. Tears cloud her vision while watching Reed interact with his niece. As they clung to each other, she notices tears streak down Jesse's face.

God, please. If you're there, please let them make it back safely. Jesse can't handle losing another loved one so quickly, and I would fall apart. Reed's been gone for too long from my life. Now, he's back, and even though we're in the middle of a nightmare, I don't want to lose him again. Please?

***

Kyle stares at the smoky remnants of what used to be his friend. The scent of burnt flesh hangs in the heavy morning air. Most of Shaun's bones remain yet the flesh is gone. Memories of all the years they'd known each other, all the cases they'd worked together, make his heart fill with sorrow. Another friend lost, another heartbreaking day.

He glances around to ensure he is still alone. "Damn you, Mike Bailey. If you can't handle this, can't control yourself in the middle of a crisis—how in the hell did you make it through the academy? It's beyond me. Musta paid someone off or sucked a few dicks. I'm glad you're leaving because I don't want to spend my remaining days trapped underground with an idiot or be the next person you blew a hole through. Bastard."

Painful emotions well up inside him. Anger, bitterness, regret, sorrow, and fear, converge together, forming a volcanic combination. He is a man of law and order, black and white, justice served for those who'd broken the law. He'd always been that way, ever since a small tyke. Just like his father, the former sheriff of Hot Spring County, Mitchell Pender. Raised with a rough hand and a boot never far from kicking his ass, Kyle learned from an early age about cause and effect. Break a rule, expect the consequences. Lie, cheat, steal, even murder, and harsh punishment awaits.

By the age of six, his heart was set on following in his gruff father's footsteps. Not the political part—he never had an interest in all the back-slapping and fake smiles that went along with running a campaign.

No, he wanted—needed—*craved*—the adrenaline rush. Wanted to be a part of making sure those who dared step out of the boundaries drawn by a civilized world paid for their misguided behavior. He loved the idea of putting on a uniform, the shiny badge, the polished shoes, the aroma of oiled leather. He yearned to be seen as a formidable foe, a man who criminals would think about before making the choice to break the law.

The fun side dishes of being a law enforcement officer were plenty. Access to various, high-powered weapons, a fast car, flashing lights, the way women looked at him when walking by. He loved everything about being a cop, yet the biggest plus was becoming friends, and eventually lovers, with Regina Parker.

He'd known Regina for years. The minute he watched her take down every single competitor at a local shooting tournament, he was hooked. The woman was strong, sexy, sure of herself. Real, down-to-earth with no tolerance for bullshit. The way the corners of her mouth curved into a seductive grin, the sheer, raw determination to devote her life to keeping others safe, was like a magnet pulling him closer from their first meeting twenty years ago.

Back then, Regina was a young, married woman, who'd recently taken on the role of Rockport's Chief of Police. Even though he knew she wasn't available, and he was living with another woman, Kyle couldn't stay away. He strolled into Rockport's tiny station one day and sweet-talked Geenie Renfro into giving him her boss's schedule and then switch shifts whenever he could with other officers, making sure he was on duty at the same time. Then, he'd casually bump into her at the gas station, or Waffle House, and best of all, be able to provide backup when Rockport PD requested assistance.

He loved Regina from a distance for years, secretly hoping she'd tire of her boring-as-a-door husband, Fred. He certainly never wished any harm on the man and felt a twinge of guilt when Fred died in a car accident.

Of course, he pushed the guilt aside, determined to be the strong shoulder Regina needed to lean on. And that's exactly what he did, though he never made a move, only offered a sympathetic ear and friendly face for her to look at while venting. Kyle waited for her to reach out and seek a different course for their relationship, and when she finally did, he'd been the happiest man in Arkansas.

He'd come close to getting married once, and had been looking at rings, but everything changed after Regina Parker burst into his world, overtook his heart, and he knew he'd never truly love another like he did the feisty woman. After letting his heart get tangled up in Regina's, he ended the long-term relationship with his girlfriend, moved out of her house, and took up residence in a small apartment. His bed didn't stay cold for too long, but the bodies warming it were exactly that—bodies with no emotional connection.

He'd developed a strong friendship with Geenie Renfro and took her shopping with him to assist in picking out the perfect engagement ring nearly two months ago.

The memories, the worries, the overwhelming sense of dread, threaten to consume his mind. He'd never hear Regina's voice again, laugh at her wicked sense of humor, hold, or kiss her, and most importantly, have the one person he trusted more than any other he'd known by his side while the world ends. The crushing agony is seconds away from sending him over the edge.

"Okay, can't do this now. She's gone, fool. Gone because you didn't protect her."

"That's quite a load of guilt you're carrying there, Kyle. Sure you need to?"

Spinning around, shocked he hadn't heard anyone approach, he lets out a huff of air when spotting Walter about ten yards away. He lowers the rifle. "You sure are one sneaky bastard, Walt. I'll give you that. Learn that little trick in the military?"

Walt walks over and studies Shaun's smoldering remains. "Yeah, and a lot of other things, too. One that might help you, if you don't mind me offering a bit of advice, is you can't live in the past. We can learn from history so we don't repeat it but that's it. There's no button to push for a restart if you ain't too fond of the present."

"You sure? Because if there is, I'd cut off my left nut to find it. Guaranteed. Slice that puppy right off."

"Best not be talking about losing body parts nowadays, Kyle. It can become a reality way too quick."

"Knew I always liked you, Walt. Our senses of humor are similar. So, since you're out here, I'm assuming that means I'm holding up the party?"

"Yep. We're all set to go. Reed, Bailey, and Allsop are on their way to the Humvees."

Kyle casts a final glance back at Shaun. "Let's hit it. Since I ain't got anyone to go smooch and fill with false promises I'll be back soon, I'm all yours."

Together, the men walk toward the main trail. After a few minutes, Walt clears his throat. "I'm sorry about Regina. Really."

"Me, too. Always knew the stubborn gal would go out with a big bang doing what she loved, which was trying to protect others. Just really, really wish she hadn't."

"She was something, that's for sure."

Kyle doesn't want Regina to be the focus of their discussion, so he changes topics. "You sure this is the right plan? I mean, we have no idea what we'll find once we leave here. The roads may be impassable, or full of munchers. Probably both. We're planning on driving over one hundred miles, and that's if we stick to the main roads. If we're forced to take the back ones, there's no telling how far we'll have to travel. If the highways are a cluster of dead vehicles and people, even if we somehow make it through the mess in the Humvees, I don't see the same thing happening with the big rigs. They ain't easy to maneuver on a clear stretch of road. Mountain Home is the closest town, so maybe we should just head there and raid their Walmart?"

"I wish it were that simple, Kyle. There might be some items left to pick, yet there might not. Those still alive probably already picked easy targets clean. That's why I initially thought about the warehouses. People will stick close to their locations to scavenge, you know, because of fears of traveling too far. My hope is the ones in Bentonville still have plenty of supplies. We're lucky we live in the state where Walmart's headquarters are located. If we wait until our supplies have dwindled to go get more, we'll be edgier, tired, and not thinking straight. Besides, you know another reason why we're heading that direction."

Kyle's temper flares. "Yeah, because of those chicken-shits, Bailey and Allsop. Well, Allsop ain't so bad, but Bailey is—"

"Now's not the time for that, Kyle. This ain't our call. We've got no right to make them stay, so if they're leaving, and heading in a direction that will be of use to us, then we go, too. Plain and simple."

"Plain and simple? Those words don't have a place in this fucking nightmare we're living in, Walter."

"Wrong. Life just became about two things: live or die. We do what's necessary to continue, even if it's only for one more day."

Kyle grinds his jaw, walking away before saying something he'll regret later.

Neither man speak another word while hiking the rest of the way to the Humvees. It takes less than thirty minutes for them to reach the camping area. Reed, Allsop, and Bailey stand at the back of the closest vehicle, their sharp gazes scanning the quiet forest. Lamar stands in the middle of the group, shaking hands.

Kyle furrows his brow. "I thought he was staying?"

"He is. He just helped carry gas cans. We might not find any on our way, and we sure can't travel far in these gas-guzzlers without extra fuel. I hated depleting our supply for the generators, so when a chance arises to get more, we take it."

Kyle bites his lip, wishing he'd wake up from the world's worst dream.

Ever.

"We'll take two vehicles in case one breaks down on the way." Walter addresses the group. "Bailey, you and Allsop ride with me. Reed and Kyle will follow. We'll take 14 all the way up toward Ridgedale, Missouri, then get on 65. Allsop's parents live near Table Rock, so we'll cut over to 265 and sneak in the back way. If we get lucky along the way and see an opportunity to snag some supplies, especially gas, we will. These beasts have plenty of storage room in the back."

"Sounds like a plan, Walter." Allsop nods in agreement. "Like I said earlier, if we find them, I'll convince them to come with us. Then we'll head to Bentonville, right? Hit 76, make a circle, and come down through 37 until we hit 62?"

"Exactly. The interstate will probably be a mess, so we're gonna just bypass the cluster-fuck. The back roads should be easier to pass through. If we run into trouble on the roads, we'll be able to navigate the wooded areas much easier."

Reed steps forward. "Not that I enjoy being the voice of ugly reason here, but we need to discuss a few things before heading out."

"Such as?" Walter asks.

"For one, alternate routes if every place we try is impassable, or simply too dangerous."

"And the other?" Mike Bailey looks irritated.

"How you two will handle the harsh truth. If we get close, and see the same destruction as we witnessed on the way here—"

"I'm not turning around!" Bailey's face flushes with anger. "And I'm not giving up until I know—for sure, without a doubt—what happened to my family. If that means I need to leave and go out on foot alone, I will. Don't even try to play off like you wouldn't do the same, Newberry."

"Never said I wouldn't, Mike. What I wouldn't do is risk everyone else's lives to find out. So, you just answered my question."

"Time's wasting, boys. Any other things to discuss before we head out?" Kyle interjects, ready to end the tense conversation.

"Just one more." Reed pauses and looks at each man. "Do we all agree this ain't a search and rescue mission, except for Allsop and Bailey's families? We're gonna see some things, people in need of assistance, along the way. As much as I hate to say it, we can't stop and offer help. We've got our own loved ones to think about. If we try to save everyone we come into contact with it'll just end up being our downfall. Personally, I don't plan on leaving Jane and Jesse up here alone. I plan on coming back in one fully intact piece. Is it safe to assume I'm not the only one thinking this way?"

"How in the world can we be so callous?" Bailey explodes. "All of us, except Walter here, are cops! We're trained to help, and you want us to just turn a blind eye? That's wrong, Newberry."

"Were cops. Past tense; were being the operative word, Bailey. Stop living in the old world!" Kyle's temper gets the best of him. "Did the last few days wipe away the memories of what happened in Malvern? Those people we tried to help, our friends and neighbors, mind you, they bolted; they didn't appreciate the help and ran like frightened sheep at the first sign of trouble. We're not helping anyone else, especially strangers. Period. It's too risky, and I'm done sticking my neck on the chopping block for ungrateful fools. That's the harsh world we live in now, so pull your head out of the past. If you don't wake up to this new reality, a *thing* might eat it in the present, or you'll fuck-up again and shoot one of us."

"Pender, you're an asshole." Bailey lunges.

Kyle is ready, delivering one solid punch. Bailey goes down after he unleashes his anger directly into Mike's chin. He grins, ready for the piece of shit to stand back up just to be knocked down once more.

"Keep your voices down, idiots. Dead ears might be listening." Walt steps over to Bailey. "Okay, you two done? Got it all outta your system, Kyle?"

"I could go another round or two. Doubt he could, though. That was for Shaun. The next would be for pure pleasure."

"You always were a prick, Pender. That ain't changed." Bailey rubs his jaw. "Yeah, I'm done."

"Okay then, back to our original topic. Though it's a tough pill to swallow, Reed and Kyle are correct." Walt's voice is firm. "We can't deviate from our plan. Can't let our emotions get to us. Stop poking the hornet's nest of past mistakes! Those still in that cave up yonder, they need us to return. So no, Reed. I don't plan on playing hero. We go, help Bailey and Allsop, then grab what we can and return. That's the mission. Time to move out."

Kyle and Reed head toward their Humvee, while Walter walks toward his. Bailey and Allsop don't move.

Bailey clears his throat. "It's not our mission, Walt. We're not in the same headspace yet. Ya'll have your loved ones around—"

"Not all of us, remember?" Kyle sneers. "Some *died* so your sorry asses could live."

Bailey ignores Kyle's outburst. "We'll go alone. If we find our families, we know our way back. We can't ignore others, and you know we'll run across some on the way. It's that simple. We'll assist those we can."

"Death sentence." Kyle glares at him, angered by his stupidity.

"I ain't running a bed and breakfast, boys." Walt pauses in mid-stride. "You and your kin—should you find them—are welcome to return. However, don't even entertain the notion of bringing strangers back. If you do, ya'll will have to set up tents in the woods. I'm not risking the lives of my loved ones. Ya'll sure this is the way you want to end things?"

Bailey and Allsop exchange glances.

Kyle senses their answer before either man speaks.

"Yeah, we're sure. Thanks for all you've done, Walter, but we ain't quite ready to let go of who we used to be just yet. Safe journeys."

Walter shifts directions, stopping next to Reed. "Same to you, boys. Hope you find your families."

Bailey and Allsop turn and climb inside the Humvee. After backing out, they head down the road.

"Well, that didn't go quite as planned. Guess we'll be heading straight to Bentonville now, huh?" Reed shakes his head. "Kinda glad because I never liked Branson. Tourist towns make me cringe."

"Yep." Walt's gaze remains on the vehicle until it is gone. "They're on a fool's quest, that's for sure. We all know they ain't gonna find shit out there but death and destruction."

"Ain't gonna miss either of them." Kyle adjusts his belt. "Stupid people won't survive much longer, and they'll just bring down those around them when they fall."

"Kyle!"

"Sorry, Reed, but it's the truth. Bailey already took Shaun's life. Which one of us would've been next? And Allsop? We'll, he's always been a dreamer—a man with his head in the clouds. Hope he crashes back to reality soon, or he'll just end up being a corpse, roaming around the countryside, looking for his next meal."

"Nice, Kyle. Real nice." Reed frowns.

Climbing inside the truck, Kyle settles into the driver's seat. "Truth always hurts, Reed. Always. Cuts to the bone of the matter, leaving the rest of the shit behind in a big, ugly pile. Let's go. I'll take the first shift driving."

Reed and Walter remain silent as they settle into the Humvee. Kyle knows his words were harsh, but he also knows both men are thinking the same thing. He sees it on their faces.

To lighten the mood, recalling how the horrible rendition of "My Girl" eased some of the tension in the group, Kyle belts out "Better Run Through the Jungle" by Creedence Clearwater Revival. In seconds, Reed and Walter joined in, and the trio headed down the road toward Hell.

He wonders if they will ever return, or if this suicide mission is their last hurrah.

Chapter 9 - Running on Empty

"COOPER? WAKE UP. We've got a problem. Several, actually."

"What's wrong, Teresa?" His nerves immediately shift to high alert. Glancing around, he realizes it is late morning, they are in the woods, and Mason isn't anywhere in sight. "Where's Mason? And where the hell are we?"

"Mason? Not a clue. We're somewhere in Oklahoma, about thirty miles from Claremore. At least, that's the last road sign I remember passing."

Climbing to the front seat, he joins Teresa. "Claremore? That's way off the route."

"Excuse me for trying to pick a road that wasn't full of the fucking dead! I had no choice but to get off 75 last night. The highways were jammed with cars and corpses. How you slept through all the twists and turns I have no idea. Mason damn near pissed himself until I stopped at this rest area and hid in the woods."

"Exhaustion does that to a person. I'd been up for two days straight." He rubs the sleep encrusted in the corners of his burning eyes. "You mentioned several problems. What else is wrong?"

Teresa points at the gas gauge. "We're running on fumes and only have one can left. The three other cans are gone. So is my gun."

"What the hell? Do you think Mason took them?"

"No, I think maybe a dead person decided to spare our lives and just rob us while we all were sleeping." Teresa's glare could have melted steel. "They got tired of shambling around and needed gas for an abandoned car they stumbled upon."

"I see getting some rest didn't help your foul mood." He scans the area for any signs of Mason. "Of course, my question was a stupid one, so forgive me. I still have sleep cobwebs inside my head."

"Yeah, obviously. Look, the kid went on a suicide mission for gas. I get that, but the chances of him finding any, or making it back here alive, are pretty much nil. I say we fill up the tank with the remaining gas and head out."

Cooper turns his gaze back to her, aware she's suffering from major trauma—hell, they all are—but the harshness in her voice and words make him cringe. He's seen what she is capable of and has no doubts she'd kill again.

Leaning over, he snatches the keys from the ignition. "I'm not leaving him. End of story."

A pair of defiant, dark eyes stare back. "Really? Mighty big turnaround there, Chief Hollingsworth. You didn't have a problem leaving the kid behind in Steamboat, so what now? We sit here as live bait, waiting until one of those things finds us, while praying the little nerd returns? Great plan."

It takes all his intestinal fortitude to remain calm. Never, in his entire life, has he considered striking a woman, but Teresa's defiance and hateful attitude makes his fingers twitch.

"I get it. You've been through some major shit. Not only did you travel far and endured horrors I can't imagine, but you didn't go willingly. Those men hurt you, and I really am sorry. Rapists and child molesters are monsters and I believe they deserved to pay, dearly, for their actions, so I'm not going to say a thing about what you did to them. Hell, I applaud you. What I won't tolerate is your callous attitude toward me or Mason. We saved your life, or did you forget that? He's just a kid for Christ's sake! Yes, I left him behind because he *wanted* to stay. It wasn't my call to make him come with us. I don't force people to do what I think is best for them. Didn't back then, and don't now."

"Really? You just took the keys away, which forces me to stay with you."

"Bullshit. You want to leave? Take your chances out there alone? Fine. Go. Just remember, there's only one gun and vehicle left, and I ain't giving them up, so you'll be unarmed and on foot."

"Which leaves me little choice."

"There are always choices, Teresa; the trick is learning to pick the right one. The safe one. The one that lets you live another day. Now, are we done with this? I hope so, because I need to go find Mason so I can get back on the road. I've got to get home and find my children."

Teresa's mouth drops open. "Are you insane?"

"Probably. The last few days pretty much wiped away the remaining traces of sanity. I woke up to a nightmare, just like you. Watched dead people eating live ones, had to shoot my wife, and have seen shit on this journey that's probably turned my hair white. All I care about is getting home and keeping you two idiots safe. You coming or staying? Your choice."

The shift in her demeanor is lightning fast. The tightness in her face relaxes as her dry lips curve into a sexy grin. "Let's stay here, Cooper. We've got some alone time, now. How long has it been since you've been with a woman? Considering we don't know if we'll live another day, maybe we should—"

"Back up your horses, girl. I've already seen what you're capable of when a man's pants are around his legs. I'd prefer to keep my boys intact. Besides, I'm a married man."

Unfazed by the words, Teresa leans closer. "Not anymore."

"This act may work on younger men, but not a seasoned one like me. I've had my fair share of women come on to me over the years, and I've always passed on the offers. I loved my wife and still do, so dial down your act. Save it for someone stupid enough to fall for it. I'm heading out. Last chance."

"God, I've always hated cops. At least that's one thing that hasn't changed during this mess. You're a tough cookie, I'll give you that. Or, maybe, you're too old to get it up? Didn't remember to pack a little blue pill?"

"You're the tough one, Teresa." Despite the tension inside the cab, he chuckles. "Your tenacity will keep you alive, I just know it. Now, I'm leaving to go find the boy. If you stay, lock the doors."

He doesn't give her a chance to respond and opens the passenger door, stepping out into the bright sunlight. Pulling the gun from the holster, he scans the area for any signs of movement, sees nothing, and turns his attention to the ground, searching for Mason's tracks.

The driver's door opens and shuts. Teresa mutters under her breath in Spanish. He figures she is calling him every cuss word she knows.

He doesn't trust the woman, so he keeps her in his line of vision. "Do you remember seeing a gas station on your drive last night?"

"Yeah, about three or four miles that way." Teresa points west. "Mason noticed, too. He wanted to stop and see if the pumps worked, but I didn't."

There is an underlying sense of fear in her words. She puts on a tough act, but she is scared, too. "Don't blame you one bit. You did just fine, girl. Just fine. Come on, Mason went west, too."

"Esto es un error."

"You keep your eyes on the woods, and if you see anything, please warn me in English." He walks alongside Mason's footprints. "I only took one year of Spanish in high school, and that was ages ago."

Teresa snorts yet doesn't speak.

He aims the key fob behind him, clicks once, and locks the SUV. As he follows Mason's steps, he prays the kid is still alive. Not only will he feel awful the kid snuck away without him hearing a thing, but the thought of riding the rest of the way to Arkansas alone with Teresa makes his guts knot up. She is dangerous. He needs another set of eyes on her.

What was Mason thinking? This is not the time to start acting like a hero. He should have waited until we woke up and they all went together. Why did he make such a stupid decision?

A sickening thought races through his mind. He stops, waiting for Teresa to do the same. After about five steps, she realizes he isn't moving and stops.

Turning back around to face him, Teresa grins seductively. "Change your mind?"

Anger erupts from inside his chest. "It was your idea, wasn't it? Used your wiles to whip the boy into a sexual frenzy, urged him to do it. Right?"

Teresa's smile disappears. Her face turns to cold marble.

He aims the gun at her temple. "Answer me! The idea wasn't Mason's, was it?"

"I don't know what you're talking about."

Closing the gap between them, he stops when less than five feet away, studying every facial movement.

Teresa stands her ground, eyes defiant.

"You better hope we find him alive. If we don't, I'll go back on my promise, blow your fucking brains out, and leave your corpse on the side of the road."

"You're wrong. It was his idea!" Teresa whines. "I tried to change his mind, but he wouldn't listen."

"Liar."

"I'm not lying! He talked about it while you were sleeping, right after we stopped. I told him no, and to wait until daylight, then we could all go. Do you really think I'd give him my gun, leaving me defenseless in a vehicle with a man I don't know? Not just no, but hell no. I woke you up the second I realized he was gone."

"When we find him, you best hope his story matches yours. If it doesn't then today will be your last day alive. Guaranteed. Keep walking and keep your foul-mouth shut. Got it?"

Teresa nods, turns, and continues forward. Lowering the gun, he follows, waffling back and forth on the pros and cons of killing her dead in her tracks.

***

"Did you hear that?" Teresa whispers.

Cooper freezes, and so does Teresa. She stares at four cars on the side of the road about forty feet ahead of them. Two SUVs, a small sedan, and one truck, are tangled together. It isn't the first time they've come across multi-vehicle accidents, and it certainly won't be the last.

He searches her face for any trickery or deception, and the hairs on his neck and arms stand erect. Teresa isn't joking. Her eyes are wide with fear.

He hadn't heard a sound other than a few crows when they first started walking. They've been on the move for nearly thirty minutes and had yet to see or hear a soul. Cocking his head, he strains to detect any noise.

A faint scratching sound up ahead makes his heart pound. Teresa nods her head, indicating she hears it, too, and points toward a mashed sedan.

Squinting in the bright sun, he searches for any movement in and around the vehicles. Beams of sunlight bounce off the windshields, making it difficult to see.

Teresa snaps her fingers and points toward the trees. Hot saliva fills his mouth.

Two gas cans are on the ground.

Motioning for her to stay put, he moves toward the wrecked vehicles. He is about ten feet away when he hears them.

The hissing, grunting noises erupt from the cab of the truck and one of the SUVs. Stopping, he plants his feet, ready for them to attack. Seconds tick by, and though their racket increases in volume, they remain inside the vehicles.

They're either restrained by their seatbelts, so mangled from the accident their legs don't work, or they haven't figured out how to open doors. Okay, steady. Mason's gotta be close.

Rounding the back end of the truck, he nearly gasps when spotting Mason on the ground next to the gas tank, the gun about three feet away from his outstretched hand.

Fighting the urge to call out his name, he dashes to the other side of the kid, praying he isn't about to see the boy as a zombie. A sigh of relief escapes—no blood; no visible wounds; no bluish lines on his face.

Crouching down, he covers Mason's mouth with his hand. "It's Cooper. Can you hear me?"

Mason's eyes flutter open. The stench of fear rolls off him in waves.

"We ain't alone, so don't yell. You hurt?" Mason shakes his head, so Cooper removes his hand. "Can you walk?"

"Yeah."

"Then move your ass. We gotta get. Now."

Gravel crunches from behind them. Spinning around, ready to shoot at an unholy monstrosity, he hesitates upon seeing Teresa.

She bends down and picks up Mason's gun. "Did you get some gas?"

"Yeah. I was filling the third one when—"

"Ain't no time for that now! Move!" Cooper grumbles.

Mason scrambles to his feet, and the three of them move away from the wreck. The creatures inside the vehicles pound on the windows. Glass shatters.

"Get the gas. Now!" Teresa yells.

"Oh, shit, wait!" Cooper realizes what she's about to do and grabs Mason by the collar, fleeing in the opposite direction.

"Five seconds. Four." Teresa scrambles backward with each word. "Three; two; one!"

Teresa fires, hitting the gas-soaked ground. The explosion knocks them all to the ground. The heat is intense as plumes of fire and smoke shoot tens of feet into the air. The eerie sounds of the grumbling dead cease.

"Holy shit!" Mason brushes dirt from his hair.

Ears still ringing from the blast, Cooper rises, brushing dirt and debris off his pants. Teresa does the same and walks toward them. His nerves zoom into overdrive. Yanking Mason up, he steps in front of him. "Don't move."

"What? Why?"

"Because she's dangerous. She almost got you killed. Twice in one fucking day!"

"Twice? What do you mean?"

"Don't lie for her, son. She sent you out here."

Mason tugs on his sleeve. "It was my idea, I swear. I, uh, wanted to impress her. You know, show her I wasn't a weak nerd?"

He isn't sure if he should laugh or slap the kid across the head to knock some sense back into his brain. "I forgot what it's like to be seventeen. No rational thoughts at all. Everything's controlled by the dick. You're damn lucky you've still got one, boy. Damn lucky. I wouldn't recommend pointing it in her direction. Don't you remember what she did to the last man we saw her with? Trust me, she's not the kind of woman you want to impress."

"They were hurting her. She did what she had to do to survive. I'm not like them. She'll see. Besides, it's not like there's a lot of women to pick from anymore. I'd like to experience sex before I croak."

Cooper bites his lower lip as Teresa joins them.

"We should get those two containers and leave. If others are close by, they'll be drawn to the noise."

"Should've thought about that before you blew them to kingdom come."

Ignoring Cooper's comment, Teresa looks at Mason. "Why weren't you moving? You don't look injured."

"I, uh, well, guess my first attempt at siphoning gas wasn't such a success." Mason's cheeks flush bright red. "I got the first two filled and had a bit of trouble with the third."

"You didn't know they were inside, did you?" Cooper asks. Mason shakes his head. "On the third attempt, you heard them, probably right around the time you were sucking out gas. Right?"

"Yeah. I choked on it. Guess I hyperventilated and fainted. So much for being a hero, huh?"

"We've got two more cans of gas, so yeah, you're a hero." Teresa smiles.

"Let's go get your hard-earned treasures and head back." Cooper releases a heavy sigh. "We've still got a lot of miles to cover."

They walk away from the burning vehicles back toward the SUV. Mason retrieves the gas cans. Cooper watches yet in silence, holding his tongue for the moment, but the second Teresa is out of earshot, he'll have a long talk with the boy. Set him straight on the kind of woman she is and to stay sharp around her before she sinks her teeth into him.

Literally.

After ten minutes into their hike back to the vehicle, Cooper can no longer contain the question niggling in the back of his mind. "Mason? What did you use to siphon gas with?"

"The emergency kit had an air compressor. I cut the hose off."

"Geek Squad, that was smart thinking, but did it ever occur to you we might need the air compressor later? We've only got one spare tire. What if we blow one, replace it, then start losing air from another?"

"I, well, guess I figured gas was the priority. Can't blow a tire if we aren't moving."

Tamping down his frustration, he takes a deep breath. "From here on out, we work as a group. No going off playing hero unless we all agree and go. Got it?"

"Sure thing, Chief!" Mason nods.

The sound of pride in the kid's voice makes Cooper shake his head. Yes, he needs to have a talk with the naïve boy.

Soon.

"Teresa said we aren't far from the Arkansas border. With three tanks of gas, we should be good, right?" Mason asks.

"Maybe. Depends on what kind of trouble we run into. This area ain't heavily populated, but the rest of our drive will be."

"Don't worry, Chief. We'll make it. We've come this far, and I'll be honest, I didn't think we'd make it out of Colorado. I was wrong, so that means there's hope. We'll make it to your kids. No doubts."

The mention of his children sends waves of anger thrumming through his chest. The frustration he's held inside bursts out. "We won't if either of you keep making stupid, spur-of-the-moment decisions! I'm tired, hungry, and pissed off. I don't need to be sidetracked with worrying about saving your asses! Yeah, we've been lucky so far, but luck runs out. Always. From now on, we don't push it any longer. Think before acting, not the other way around. If you don't, we'll all end up like those burnt corpses back there. Got it?"

Mason and Teresa both while looking at the ground rather than his face. No one speaks another word the rest of the fifteen minutes they walk.

Once back at the SUV, Cooper unlocks the doors. Mason fills the gas tank then climbs inside, pride wounded, and face flushed. Reaching underneath the driver's seat, he hands the kid a bottle of water. "Drink, but not too fast. Keep your eyes out for any signs of trouble. Both of you."

Two heads bob in agreement, so he eases out onto the road and headseast, thankful to be alive, and closer to home.

I'm coming, kids. I'm coming, if these two don't screw up again.

Chapter 10 - Time to Fly Away

Thursday, December 25th – 1:15 p.m. – Central Standard
Time

"ANYONE REALIZE WHAT today is?"

"Yeah, Christmas. Ho-fucking-ho. No presents this year, other than the biggest lump of coal ever." Kevin deadpans. "Feels just like it did when I was a kid. Santa couldn't get to our house back then either. Just like he didn't get through all this rock. Instead of Jolly Ol' Saint Nick, Krampus appeared. But you know what, Doc? We're safe here. If magical elves can't penetrate these walls, nothing can."

"We aren't safe here, Kevin. Not for much longer." Everett adds.

"Jesus, Kevin. When did you become such a whiner?" Clive slams an empty water bottle onto the table. "I sure am sick of hearing you piss and moan."

"Picked it up from your mom, asshole. Right after I—"

Kevin and Clive are at each other's throats before Everett has time to blink. Dirk and Denaryl jump from their spots and pull them apart while he watches from his perch at the end of the table with a heavy knot of dread coiling inside his stomach.

"Now it's just like Christmas at my house. Every year, there was always at least one fight." Dirk yanks Clive off Kevin. "The only difference is it's not me and my brother going at each other. I'll repeat what my father used to say: Next one out of line gets a boot in the ass. I'm not kidding. We don't have the luxury of acting like hormonal twelve-year-olds."

"Sorry, guess that wasn't the appropriate time to bring up the subject of Christmas." Everett clasps his shaking hands together. "It's just, well, I was tired of rehashing the same topic and listening to all of you argue. Believe me, gentlemen, Christmas is my least favorite time of the year. The last thirteen sucked, and this one tops them all."

"Actually, it's rather appropriate today is Christmas. A time for new beginnings, right Doc?"

"Something like that, though I've been waiting for a ray of hope for a long time. No beams of happiness are around."

"Enough theatrics, all of you!" Denaryl's deep baritone booms from across the room. "Doc, I want to know if you are certain this is a real threat."

"Wow, he speaks! You haven't said ten words since we've been here, Dee. Now you decide to join a conversation?"

"Warton, I've kept quiet because no one could get a word in around you. Your mouth's always busy flapping enough for all of us. Stop spouting your bullshit and interrupting questions asked to another. Doc?"

Everett sighs while raising his gaze to meet Denaryl Rice's warm, chocolate brown eyes. He's always liked the kid because he senses another damaged soul behind the tough facade. "I'm ninety-nine percent positive."

"Only ninety-nine percent? Maybe we should go check out the facility, you know, just to be sure?" Clive rubs the back of his neck. "There could still be workers there."

"So, you're volunteering to go to a nuclear reactor and check it out, Winters? Hope so because there's no way I'm going." Drake's tone is full of irritation. "Too risky. That one percent window don't mean shit."

"Nothing in this world is one hundred percent, except dying." Everett interrupts, hoping to keep the two men from exploding at each other. "Even that's changed because people are reanimating. Arkansas Nuclear One is just a ticking time bomb. I'd bet my life on it, no hesitation. Depending upon certain factors, it will be days, or weeks, before meltdown."

"Not years? Doc, are you sure?" Dirk asks.

Everett nods.

"Then we don't risk a mission there. Period," Dirk says with finality.

"You're going to trust the man who started all this?" Kevin looks incredulous. "Are we really going to put our lives in this old fool's hands? What if he's wrong?"

Denaryl cuts his gaze from Everett's face to Kevin's. "We all know you disagree with the decision to leave. Not all of us feel the same way. So, here's my vote, if it even matters. We go. I don't care where, just get the fuck outta here before this shit happens. At least with this catastrophe, we've got some warning. A slow death from radiation exposure does not interest me at all."

Clive throws up his hands. "Oh, but you're willing to risk a quick death after getting torn apart by decaying corpses, Dee?"

"If it means I won't be trapped underground and slowly rotting away while poison courses through my veins, yes. A few days of healthy freedom with a quick ending certainly sounds better than what awaits us here."

"What about Dr. Berning's research?" Drake questions. "Where in the world could we go that's safe and has a lab?"

"Dr. Berning, would you like to answer Drake's question?"

Everett rises from the chair, wishing Dirk hadn't asked him to expound. He doesn't want to dump yet another pile of awful news on the already strung-out men, though he knows there isn't a choice.

"Go ahead, Doc. Kevin won't interrupt, right?" Dirk's words aren't spoken as a question.

Kevin grunts an answer while slumping into a chair.

Everett clears his throat. "At the present our biggest threat is radiation. If we remain here and I continue working on a cure, I'll need more specimens. Some of you would have the task of acquiring them, which not only poses danger from the dead, but exposure to radiation. Nuclear reactors require power to run the cooling pumps. If they no longer function, meltdown occurs. Radiation cannot be detected by human senses, and we don't have any equipment on site to alert us when it's in the air. We wouldn't know we've been exposed until it's too late."

"What about the bio suits? Can't we use them?" Clive asks.

"They would protect from some radioactive contamination, yes. However, we only have four left, and there's no way to decontaminate them, or even know, if you've been exposed. It's too risky to stay here. We're downwind and less than one-hundred miles away. In other words, sitting ducks. When we run out of supplies, everything around us topside will be contaminated and unusable."

Dirk cocks his head. "I seem to remember during training that the safe-zone area is fifty miles, not one hundred."

"That's a minimum safe distance. Other factors come into play, such as the wind pattern and weather. Winds tend to travel west to east, which throws us right into the path. Remember what happened in Japan at Fukushima? Radiation—right this very minute—is still spreading across the Pacific. When a plant is damaged and can't cool the towers, a meltdown occurs. Not if, but when."

"Maybe the radiation will cure the zombies?" Kevin shrugs his shoulders.

Dirk scowls. "Warton!"

"Sorry, but some levity is needed. This is some heavy shit we're talking about! Walking corpses in one hand, radiation poisoning in the other. Some world we live in now. Fuck!"

Everett addresses Kevin directly. "I know, and believe me, I don't like being the person each of you cringe at every time I open my mouth. My news is never good. So, here's the outcome of my calculations, which isn't good news, either. Finding a cure will take time. Not only are more specimens needed to do so, but I haven't figured out the type of fungi we're dealing with, and even if I'm successful at figuring that out and manage to concoct some sort of anti-zombie formula, it will benefit only those of us not contaminated. The dead have no hope. Then there's figuring out a way to create enough for other survivors, how to get it to them, and so forth. Those things can—*need*—to be done in a safe zone. This location doesn't qualify. Let's all hope we aren't the only ones working on a cure. Surely there are some people left in the world doing the exact same thing."

The men all speak at once, so Dirk holds up a hand, silencing them. "Look, stop bitching, and realize how lucky we are. Dee's a pilot. He can fly the Gulfstream sitting in the hangar not far from Dr. Thomas' place. We leave, drive to the hangar, and fly the friendly skies to someplace without a nuclear power plant. The only thing we need to do now is figure out where to go."

"Okay, sure! Let me just go grab my map of the world listing all the locations of nuclear reactors." Kevin snaps. "Then, we'll play pin the tail on the country."

"There's one in the library at Dr. Thomas' estate."

"Are you sure, Doc?" Dirk raises an eyebrow.

"Yes. I remember passing by it numerous times when I couldn't sleep and went to the library to read."

Dirk sets his jaw. "Then it's settled. We pack up and leave tomorrow at 0800."

"What about the group of survivors we ran into? Do we warn them? Take them with us?" Everett asks. The thought of leaving the first people they'd encountered makes his stomach sour.

"No. Too many of them. The Gulfstream only seats twelve. I know it's a death sentence for them, but it cannot be helped. They'd be forced to pick who stays and who goes, so they'll be better off all dying together." Dirk turns his focus to the other men. "Warton, Denton, Rice, and Winters—you all secure the place and remove the crispy pilots out front. Make sure to render them into ashes. Dr. Berning and I will handle the lab. Any questions?"

"Yeah, just one." Kevin glares at Everett, eyes pulsating with anger. "Why couldn't you have told us this earlier, Berning? You know, like before we left the estate and hid inside this fucking place like frightened bats? We could have simply hopped on the plane back then and headed somewhere safe."

"I didn't realize the finality of what happened at the time, Mr. Warton. Forgive me for not handling this nightmare with finesse. Seeing the dead walking around kind of messed things up inside my head."

"Warton—shut up. Enough already." Dirk's voice is low and menacing. "Stop pointing the finger of blame at Dr. Berning. I had a much bigger hand in this than he did, so if you've got a problem with him, you do with me, too."

"What the fuck are you talking about, Dirk?" Kevin's eyes fill with confusion.

"I'm the one who decided to go to Laredo alone, remember? I forced Dr. Berning to leave Laredo the night I rescued him *without* the formula and his notes during a heat of battle decision. My options were to let him get shot by wasting precious seconds to snatch the bag or save his life. I chose the latter, so here we are.

Neither of us even remotely entertained the idea this disaster would be the end results, so lay the fuck off him and start packing. Now."

Kevin, Drake, and Clive leave without saying another word. Everett's mouth gapes open, stunned into silence at Dirk's words. He appreciates the man sticking up for him.

"It's going to happen everywhere there's a reactor, right?" Denaryl takes a deep breath. "All over the world?"

Everett nods.

"Jesus, the whole world is fubared in more ways than one." Denaryl wipes sweat from his brow. "Hurry up and figure out where I need to fly because I'm ready to get into the clouds."

Denaryl exits the room, leaving a bewildered Everett staring at his rigid back. "Dirk, what does fubared mean?"

"Fucked up beyond all recognition."

"Quite the appropriate acronym."

"Yeah, quite. Come on, Doc. Let's get moving so we won't be in the same boat."

Chapter 11 - Christmas in a Cave
Thursday, December 25th – 2:15 p.m. – Central Standard Time

"LAMAR, AREN'T YOU gonna eat? You haven't touched your food."

Looking up from his plate, Martha's words bring Lamar back to the present conversation. "Sorry, not too hungry. I'll eat later. Promise."

Martha frowns. "No, you'll eat now, and let out whatever's crawling around inside your head. Remember, we're supposed to share our thoughts, and it's obvious you've got some rolling around. Talk. We're listening."

He isn't the kind of man given to bouts of emotion. After his wife died of cancer twelve years prior, he shut himself off, pouring all his efforts into being a prepper, filling the lonely hours after work with research, and the companionship with the others in the prepper group, to satisfy his needs.

How is he supposed to tell them what he overheard in the woods yesterday? The three women and a young, injured boy are already teetering on the edge of hysteria. Jane spent the entire night pacing back and forth, only stopping to stare at the entrance. Martha busied herself by doting on Turner, while Jesse talked non-stop. All of them are worried about their loved ones, so how can he dump the news?

The worry about a nuclear disaster has been a nagging thought in the back of his mind since yesterday. When everything went down in Malvern and their escape to the mountains, Lamar was so mentally and physically exhausted, he'd forgotten all about the dangers lurking in Russellville. He'd been too busy grappling with the knowledge the dead were walking and interested in eating the flesh of others.

Now, he is beyond terrified.

"Lamar? You're as pale as a ghost. What's going on?" Jane's brows furrow with worry.

"Nothing. Just thinking about how this is the weirdest Christmas ever. Eating soup and canned peaches inside a cave. Glad I'm not alone. Grateful to be surrounded by a fine group of people. Things like that."

Turner shifts positions, grunting with the effort. "I call bullshit. You don't just look like a ghost; you look like you've seen one. Come on, Lamar. We're family. All each other's got, so share. There ain't none of us gonna judge you for whatever's on your mind."

He rises, unwilling to look at the four, worried faces staring at him for answers. He cannot lie unless he turns away. "Just thinking about Bertha, that's all. I miss her, yet I hate myself for thinking I'm glad she died before all this happened. Bertha was like you, Jesse."

"You mean claustrophobic?"

"Yes. She wouldn't have lasted but maybe five minutes in here. So, I feel like an ass for being glad she's gone."

Lamar chokes up, biting his lip to keep from crying. Someone stands and walks toward him. A warm hand touches his shoulder.

"Don't beat yourself up for thinking that way, Lamar." Martha whispers. "It doesn't mean you don't miss your wife. It means you loved her dearly and realize she couldn't have handled this situation. Come on now, eat. We all need to stay strong and healthy if we're gonna get through this together."

His heart breaks and the words tumble out. "We ain't gonna get through this, Ms. Martha."

"Of course we will, Lamar!"

Pulling away, he turns and faces the group. "Not here we won't."

"What? Why?" Confusion spreads across Turner's face. "We're safe as kittens inside this big cave."

He shakes his head while tears stream down his face. "God, I swear, I don't know how to say this, but we aren't."

Jesse strides across the floor, grabs his shoulders, and forces him to make eye contact. "Lamar? If you know something we don't, spit it out. We've made it this far after losing everything, and almost everyone, we know. Whatever it is, we'll face it together. Say what's on your mind."

"Arkansas Nuclear One."

Jane and Martha both gasp, but Jesse and Turner look confused.

"Oh, dear Jesus. I forgot all about that place!" Martha wrings her hands together.

Lamar nods. "So did I, for a few days. Yesterday, on my way back from seeing the boys off, I was slapped back into reality."

"How?" Turner asks.

"I heard a noise and followed it. Snuck up on two of those men we ran into the other day. You know, the one's in the underground lab?"

Everyone nods.

"They were down by the graves, burning bodies, grousing about leaving. One of them was on a tear, complaining about their doctor, and how he should have thought about the meltdown and radiation exposure before they decided to come this way."

"Radiation? Meltdown? I don't understand, Lamar." Jesse whispers.

"Arkansas Nuclear One is a reactor, and without power to keep it cool, it will go into meltdown. Radiation will be released and head right this way."

Martha and Jane look like they are seconds from passing out. Jesse backs away from him and rushes to Turner's side.

"What else did you hear, Lamar?" Jane asks while pacing in small circles.

"They're planning on leaving tomorrow morning and flying somewhere safe. Didn't hear where just that they're going. Apparently, their doctor realized the dangers, too, and they ain't staying."

"Leaving? Tomorrow?" Jesse's voice cracks. "What about the cure he's supposed to be working on?"

"I don't know. Guess they're giving up on that, at least, for now."

"Great! Zombies and now radiation poisoning? This is insane!" Jesse whines.

"Lamar, in your research, did you study up on—?"

"Yes, Ms. Martha. Radiation was another one of my fears."

"How long before meltdown?"

"I ain't no expert, ma'am, but from what I remember reading, a few weeks. Month, tops."

"Okay, let's not panic just yet." Turner tries to sound positive, but it isn't working. "We're in a cave, which will protect us, right?"

"For a while, yes. But eventually, we'll have to venture out to find more food, and then we'll get contaminated. Or, whatever's left to scavenge will be."

Jesse appears to be on the verge of a crying jag. Instead of sobbing, she squares her shoulders, bends down, kisses Turner's forehead, and then turns her gaze toward Lamar. The steely look on her face wipes all traces of the young woman's features away. Though her hair color is different, the resemblance to her mother is downright eerie.

"We've been through too much to give up now. If those men are leaving, and have access to a plane, then they'll just take us with them."

"That's crazy, Jesse!" Jane's mouth gapes open. "We don't know them, or where they're going, and the guys aren't back yet! We can't leave without them."

Jesse points to the rifle at the end of Turner's cot. "We aren't going to, Jane. We won't give those men a choice. Our loved ones are out there, risking their lives for us. It's time we did the same. I've got a plan."

"And that is?" Lamar is shocked by Jesse's determination.

"We've got a man in need of medical assistance, and they've got a doctor. You know where their lab is, Lamar. Take me there, and I'll convince them we need help right away, or my fiancé won't make it. Then, we will take the doctor hostage, using him as leverage to wait until Uncle Reed and the rest of them return *and* take us all on that flight."

"There's no way that'll work, Jesse! They aren't stupid. Those soldiers are former Special Forces. I saw their tats. They won't let the doc go alone if they let him go at all, which means we'll have at least one, if not more, highly trained killers inside here. We can't take down that many."

Jesse grins. "They'll let him come, I guarantee it. And you're right, he won't come alone."

"Then why in the world are you smiling?"

"Because they have no idea how many of us are here, and where we're hiding." Jesse picks up a rifle. "Right, Jane? Martha? Besides, they'll be busy carrying me, after I completely freak out, overcome with worry about my fiancé."

Lamar chuckles. "You know, that just might work!"

"We don't have the luxury of 'just might', Lamar. It'll be guaranteed if the terrified fiancé *and* the distraught mother arrive, begging for help."

"No, no way, Martha. Walt would never forgive me if I let you do that."

"Ain't open for any more discussion, Lamar. Now, tell us how to get to that lab in detail while you eat. You're gonna need your strength against those goons."

***

"Sonofabit! I can't believe it." Kyle's low whisper is tinged with fury.

Reed, Walt, and Kyle stare at what used to be the warehouse. When they spotted smoke wafting in the air from the road, they feared this would be what they found. They stopped at the edge of the parking area, exhausted and angry. Chunks of debris littered the parking lot, along with countless bodies—and body parts—burned beyond recognition. The building isn't just destroyed, it is obliterated. Smoke drifts from small fires still burning inside the rubble.

His chest tightens. He cannot believe they made it to Bentonville through all the hordes of the dead and dying along the way, only to come up empty-handed. "Think there's anything left inside to salvage? Should we even try, or just turn around and go back?"

Walt rubs his temples. Reed notices the devastation all over his face. They are all running on fumes.

"The warehouse is toast, and ain't none of those trucks in shape to drive. I say we check out some of the trailers, see if anything's left inside is worth taking. If we come up with a goose egg, we'll head back. Finish clearing out that Dollar General we stopped at on the way here in Harrison. We already took out the dead wandering around inside the place, so it will be a piece of cake."

"Walt, won't they be locked? The trailers, I mean?" Kyle asks.

"Got bolt cutters in the back, so no worries."

"You see any munchers?" Kyle moves closer to the window, squinting. "All I'm seeing are dead bodies that ain't moving."

"None yet."

"Jesus, this confirms what we've all feared: the government took out everything. Shit!" Kyle slams his fist into the console. "I can't believe it. I held on to a string of hope we we're just overreacting and that this didn't happen everywhere."

Walt reaches behind the back seat, grabbing the bolt cutters. "I did too, Kyle. I surely did. Like I've always said, the government can't be trusted to watch a kitten, much less take care of its citizens. There's your proof. Not that we really needed more, but this kind of ices the cake."

Reed continues scanning the parking lot as a heavy sense of unease rumbles inside his gut. Movement about twenty feet ahead near the tree line catches his attention. Squinting, a sense of relief hits him upon realizing it is only a few stray dogs sniffing around the corpses.

"Dinner's cooked and ready, so where are all the munchers? Guess they like their meat raw."

"Kyle, your sense of humor is getting on my nerves. Have some respect, will you?" Reed snaps. "Stop acting like this is some joke. We're about to step out into Hell, which means we need to be focused."

"Easy, Reed. Easy." Kyle holds up his hands in mock surrender. "I'm freaked out, too. I just handle it differently."

"Yeah, I recall you saying humor is insanity's next of kin. I'd say you crossed over."

"If you two are done jawing, we need to lock and load. Daylight's wasting, and we've got a long day ahead of us." Walt grumbles. "We ain't got many rounds left after the nightmare in Harrison, so make your shots count. Got it?"

Reed nods while glancing at both men's clothes and then down at his own. They all look like they've bathed in blood. He lost count of how many hungry corpses they'd shot on the journey. Killing them from a distance wasn't too bad, but when they found themselves in too close and the speed of the monsters overtook them, they'd all taken out their knives. At the time, he didn't register anything, he just stabbed and sliced his way through. Thinking about it now makes his stomach rumble. The sounds and disgusting sensation of shoving metal through a skull will haunt him the rest of his life.

"Got it, Walt." Kyle points out the window. "Should we head for those three trailers right there?"

"Yep. Keep your steps quiet, head on a swivel, and use hand signals. Kyle, pull up as close as you can to that trailer there." Walt points to the right. "We'll start with that one. If we find useful items, work double-time to get this Humvee loaded. Maybe we'll get lucky and find enough salvageable items to fill this baby up. Then we get the fuck outta here."

Kyle eases forward, not even trying to dodge the crisp bodies strewn across the ground. Reed looks around, taking in everything. He notices another three dogs, bringing the total to eight. They are big, ugly looking mutts with matted fur and streaks of blood all over their coats. When he realizes they aren't just sniffing around and are eating the burned remains, he shakes his head in disgust. "We've got four-legged company over there. My guess, judging by the way they look, is they're wild. Keep an eye on them."

Walt curses. "Dogs will eat anything when hungry, even their poop. That's why I've always had a no pet policy at my house. Animals are just that—animals. Give them a reason, they'll revert to predator in a heartbeat."

"That surprises the hell outta me, Walt." Kyle laughs. "I always pictured you as the kinda guy with a passel of hunting dogs around. Learn something new every day."

Stopping within feet of the nearest trailer, Kyle reaches to shut the engine off, but Walt stops him. "No, leave it running. We might need to leave in a big hurry. Open the back and let's do this. Count of three. Ready?"

Reed swallows hard, gaze taking in another full sweep of the lot. "Ready."

Walt grabs the door handle. "One; two; three!"

The men fan out of the Humvee, Walt in the lead with the bolt cutters, Kyle in the middle, and Reed at the back, weapons high and nerves on full alert while jogging to the back of the trailer. The smell of burnt flesh makes his nose burn and eyes water.

Walt cuts through the deadbolt on the trailer doors, motioning for him and Kyle to stand guard while he opens them. The creaking metal is loud in the quiet afternoon air. His heart thunders inside his chest.

All three breathe a sigh of relief at what is inside. Boxes and boxes of canned goods, toiletries, bottled water, and dry goods, mostly undamaged.

Best Christmas presents ever!

Backing up, Reed watches the area, gun at the ready as Walt climbs inside and starts handing boxes to Kyle. The duo work in tandem loading the Humvee. The only sounds are their footfalls, light breathing, and the annoying chewing noises from the dogs chomping away on charred corpses.

Hurry up, boys! Hurry up. Something ain't right here. I can feel it. We've got enough for now—we can always hit Dollar General on the way back. We need to go, right now! I want to get back to Jane and Jesse. I want—

His internal worries are cut short by the most terrifying growl he's ever heard. The second it reaches his ears his gaze darts right.

The dogs are gone.

"Oh, shit—!"

Spinning around, his heart skips several beats. All eight of the dogs ae less than ten feet from his position. Red, foamy looking saliva drips from their muzzles. They've formed a half-circle around him, blocking all paths to run. Some have broken legs; others have holes the size of golf balls through their bodies. A few of them snarl exposing blood-covered mouths.

None of them are breathing.

Jane—here's your answer. It crosses species.

"Humvee, now!" He screams at the exact moment several lunge.

The sounds of Kyle and Walt yelling fade into white noise because in that split second of time, he knows what is about to happen. He opens fire, shooting the ones closest to Walt and Kyle, giving them a short window of opportunity to get to safety.

I promised Jane no heroics. Sorry, babe.

The dead dogs howl, descending on him so fast he cannot shoot them all. Two launch themselves into his chest, knocking him to the ground. His head smashes into the pavement with a sickening thud. Dropping the rifle, his hands find the strong neck of the one biting and snarling inches from his face.

"Walter! Shoot those mongrels! Oh, shit! Munchers to the right!" Kyle screams.

Gunfire erupts, drowning out the hellish growls of the dogs. Reed holds onto the neck of one, kicking at the others. Burning pain explodes inside his leg as one tears into his thigh muscle. He yelps in agony.

In a desperate, last-ditch attempt, he lets go with one hand, scrambling to remove the hunting knife from his waist. Just as his fingers latch onto the handle, another dog sinks its teeth into his hand. The sound of bones breaking as it rips away from his wrist elicits another scream.

Hysteria overtakes his mind. "No! Not like this!"

His terror-filled wails stop as one dog latches onto his throat. The gunshots seem distant, along with the growls from the dogs. The bright afternoon light disappears, and to his surprise, there is no more pain.

Jane. Jesse. I'm sorry.

***

"Fuck, they're on him!" Walt screams.

Jumping out from the inside of the trailer, he runs, firing several rounds at the one on top of Reed, hitting the intended target each time, yet the dog never flinches. Sliding to a stop, he takes aim at the head.

"Shoot those mongrels! Oh, shit! Munchers to the right!" Kyle yells.

A burst of rounds from Kyle's rifle sends Walt's nerves into overdrive, senses bombarded with too much sensory input. "Get them! Gotta save Reed!"

More gunshots explode behind him, and he faintly registers the fact there are too many fired in quick succession to be from Kyle alone. Pushing away the possibility others are around and helping, he homes in on the dogs.

One rips Reed's hand off while another tears a chunk of thigh muscle away. Steading his aim, he blows the head off the mutt with the hand still in its mouth. Firing again, he hits the one near Reed's leg. The monster crumples to the ground.

The dog on his chest goes for the jugular. Hands shaking from the rush of adrenaline and terror, Walt fires, but the bullet only clips the dog's ear.

It descends on Reed's neck. Blood pours from the jugular, covering the ground with a red stain of crimson. Dizziness blurs Walt's vision as horror seeps into his mind.

No. Not Reed. Dear God, not Reed.

"Left side, Walt! Left side!"

The mind-altering sorrow from watching Reed Newberry get torn to shreds by dead dogs and take his last breath, disappears at Kyle's words. Senses back, Walt jerks left, gun at his shoulder.

He is too late.

Three corpses descend on him before he can get off even one round.

"Fuck! Fuck! Fuck!" Kyle screams.

Bullets whizz all around him as his body flies backward several feet. The impact of the fall, and the weight of the creatures on top of him, knock the breath from his lungs. The stench of their foul breath and rotting bodies shut everything else from his mind. His sole focus is on survival.

Ignoring the pain as they rip flesh from his body, he screams like a banshee while snatching the Bowie knife from his side. Grabbing the rotten neck of the one chomping on his shoulder, he buries the blade into its temple, tosses the corpse to the side, and attacks the one on munching on his leg. "Die, bastard! Die again!"

In a frenzy of blood and wails of abject terror, mind beyond the point of sanity as intense pain wracks his body, he slashes and stabs at the final corpse. Pulling from reserves deep inside his mind, he latches onto its arm with one hand, intending to shove the blade up through its jaw.

He doesn't get the chance.

The creature's head explodes, courtesy of Kyle.

Craning his neck to look around, blurry vision registers more movement near him.

Kyle races over to his side. "That's the last one. Come on, we've got to get out of here. Right now."

"More coming," Walt's voice is barely above a whisper.

Burning pain, the worst he's ever felt, consumes all rational thought. He knows the bites are a death sentence. He tries pulling up images of Martha or Turner.

"No, they're gone. We got 'em all, Walt. That's our help over there. Hang tight. Let me get the bleeding stopped."

"Oh, shit. Mason—get the first aid kit!"

Walt senses another presence at his side. Forcing his eyes open, he tries to grin. "Chief Hollingsworth?"

"Yeah, Walter. It's me. Be quiet now. Save your strength. We'll get you outta here in a flash."

"He's been bitten! That means—"

"Hush, Teresa!" Cooper hisses. "Walt? Walt, come on. Stay with us, buddy. Hang on."

Walt's eyes are open, but he cannot see anything. He knows he only has mere seconds. "Take care of my family, Cooper, and me. Put me down. I ain't gonna be..."

With no more strength left to speak as convulsions wrack his body, the last thing Walter Addison hears is Kyle's voice. "No, Cooper. I'll do it. God's speed, Walter. I'm so sorry."

Chapter 12 - Deadly Negotiations

"DON'T DO THIS, honey. It's a mistake."

"No, Turner, the mistake is sitting on our asses like a bunch of frightened chickens." Jesse sets her jaw. "We're getting on that plane, no matter what."

Martha smiles. "Stop fretting, son. We've got this."

"You've got maybe an hour of daylight left, so you best scoot." Lamar urges. "I'll stand guard by the door, and when I hear y'all coming, I'll slip back inside. Me and Ms. Jane will get into position and welcome those boys right proper when they step inside."

Jesse kisses Turner's hand. "Remember, Lamar, only knock them out. If we kill them, we lose our bargaining chips. Promise?"

Lamar nods.

"I ain't killing anyone." Jane's voice is low, quiet. "It's completely against my calling, so don't worry."

"Let's do this. I'm ready to live somewhere that ain't underground anyway." Jesse smiles at Turner. "I love you. We'll be back soon. Promise."

Martha swipes a kiss on Turner's forehead, grabs a rifle and follows Jesse toward the entrance.

"Be safe. Remember, they're trained killers. Don't let your guard down even for one second."

"We won't, Lamar." Martha gives him a hug. "You stay sharp, too. We'll be back soon."

Jesse and Martha step out into the cold air, each with rifles slung over their shoulders. Martha leads the way, following Lamar's instructions toward the lab. Jesse doesn't say a word, preferring to let Martha concentrate.

Something inside her mind shifted when Walter and the others returned the night Shaun died. Though saddened by the loss, she didn't really know Shaun too well. What bothered her was the news they brought back about how all of this tied to drugs and how close she came to turning into the undead her first day in the mountains.

Heart. Her mother said she was strong and would make it because of her heart. Finally, she understands. The second she heard drugs were involved she grew up. Literally, in seconds. The cravings are gone. The reality of the world broke through the haze of sadness and sorrow, pushing past the pain and ripping away the old girl she'd been.

A new sense of determination to survive—and thrive—kicked into overdrive when Lamar told them of the other danger they faced. People she loves, and even some she doesn't, risked their lives to save hers, and it is high time she embodies her mother's spirit of service and sacrifice. She'll do whatever necessary—no matter what—to live, and be a productive, reliable member of the group.

Drugs ruined everything, not just her life. Every. Fucking. Thing. She refuses to let them control her thoughts any longer.

Martha slows her pace and whispers, "Okay, we're close. About fifty yards up yonder. Lamar said they have sensors, which have probably already picked us up. Time to start our act. Remember, we can't walk right up to the entrance. We run around like we're lost. Just follow my lead, okay?"

"Best acting job ever, coming right up."

Martha walks forward another ten feet and then starts crying. "We don't know where they are! Walt never said, just they were this way. How in the world will we find them in time?"

"It's okay, Martha. We will. Somehow. Turner needs us to stay strong. Don't give up hope."

"I can't believe the minute they leave to get supplies my son takes a turn for the worse. His fever is really high. What're we gonna do if we can't find them? I don't want my boy to die! We've already lost enough."

"It's okay, Martha. We'll find the doctor. I just know it. Turner's gonna be okay." She puts her arms around Martha's neck, hugging her while giving a quick scan of the woods. They aren't far from the lab's hidden door. Lamar said they had to have another way out, or they never would have been able to get the drop on them before.

Leaves crunch about twenty feet away. Martha stiffens; Jesse freezes, praying they are from one of the soldiers and not a corpse.

Pulling away from the embrace, Martha backs up, gaze scanning the woods, hands clasping the rifle. "Help! Please! My son needs a doctor! If you can hear me, please!"

"Ladies, enough. You're loud enough to wake the dead, which is a death sentence nowadays."

Jesse and Martha exchange glances, nerves in high alert. The male voice came from behind a large crop of boulders not far ahead.

"Oh, thank God! Please, are you the doctor? My son is dying."

"Put the weapons down and we'll talk. Nice and easy."

This is the only part of the plan Jesse hates, but there is no choice. They must play the role of frightened women. Each set their rifles on the ground and put their hands in the air.

"We mean you no harm, I swear. My fiancé, her son, Turner—he's hurt. Bad. He fell down the mountainside a few days ago, and he's not doing well. His fever spiked and he's unconscious."

"My husband, Walter, said you've got a doctor. Is that true?"

"We do, but he's busy at the moment."

Jesse takes a deep breath, steadying herself for the performance of a lifetime. "That's your answer? He's busy? Aren't we all? Busy trying to survive! You think we risked coming out here, near dark and alone, for fun? Turner's dying. We left him alone to find help! Everyone else left us to search for food. If I lose one more person, I'll go insane. Just five minutes, please?"

"If it's such an emergency, you should've brought him with you."

"His leg is broken, and some ribs! We couldn't carry him and keep an eye out for monsters. We need help, so please—oh, Martha, they're just gonna let Turner die!" Jesse sobs, crumpling to the ground.

The racket works. Two me appear from behind the boulders.

"Look, take our weapons—just please, help us!" Martha urges.

"Stop that noise, right now, or we go back inside."

"Shhh, Jesse. It's okay. They'll help us."

"Denton, go get Doc, and tell him to bring meds with him."

"You sure, Dirk?"

"Yes. Go."

Slowing her tears, Jesse glances up. The man named Denton disappears behind the boulders. The other remains, studying their faces with mild curiosity.

"You're Walter's wife?"

"Yes. This is Jesse, Turner's fiancé. We had to get help. Turner's ill, and we didn't know what else to do. Walter mentioned your name, said you were a good man. Thank you for helping us."

"Step away from your weapons, please. Can't take any chances nowadays."

Martha walks over to Jesse as Dirk picks up the rifles, securing them around his neck.

It is time for act two of Jesse's performance. She fakes hyperventilating.

"God...can't...breathe...Turner's...gonna...die!"

"No, he's not. Our doctor will be here any second. Calm down."

"Breathe, Jesse. Slow. In and out." Martha rubs Jesse's back.

Flapping her arms, Jesse yells, "Can't breathe!" and then flops onto her back, eyes closed.

"What the hell?" Dirk asks.

"Panic attack. She's had several since all this started. Lost her mom in the mess, and now she's terrified of losing my son."

"Dirk? What's going on?"

"She just fainted, that's all. Drake? See if you can wake her back up."

"Are you the doctor?" Martha asks.

Jesse keeps her eyes shut as more footfalls approach. A cold hand pats her cheek, soft at first, then with more pressure. She forces her body to remain still.

"Yes. Dr. Everett Berning. Drake tells me your son's unconscious with a high fever. For how long?"

"About two hours. We were so scared he wouldn't make it all we could think of was finding you. Thank you. Please, Dr. Berning, our cave ain't too far away."

"She's out cold." Drake rises to his feet.

"Carry her. Let's go and get this over with before night settles in. Lead the way, Mrs. Addison," Dirk instructs.

Strong arms heft Jesse from the ground. In seconds, she is slung over Drake's shoulder. Biting her lip to remain quiet, she lets her body flop around as the group treks back toward the cave.

Plan A—completed. I hope Lamar and Jane are ready for Plan B.

***

"This is it, right this way." Martha clears her throat.

The words and noise are Jesse's cue, and Lamar's, they are close. Dirk and Drake didn't speak much during the hike, but Martha and the doctor talked nonstop about Turner's injuries. Martha did a fine job explaining, recounting all the medical terminology Jane coached her to use.

"Glad you and your family decided to evacuate to a cave." Dr. Berning's breathing sounds labored. "Preppers?"

"Yes, though we certainly didn't plan on staying here forever. After what you told my husband, that's the new plan, and the reason they went on a supply run. We only had enough stored here for three months. We used up a lot of medical supplies when Turner got hurt. Please, hurry. He's all alone in there. We've been gone over an hour."

Jesse can tell from the footsteps Drake is bringing up the rear. Opening her eyes, she peeks around, grimacing in the dark. She can't see shit, but she knows they must be close to the entrance. Martha was to say the words when about thirty feet away, giving Lamar enough time to slip back inside and close the door without the sound of the grinding metal reaching their position.

"Look, there's the door!" Martha's voice rises an octave.

"Doorway's too low." Drake curses. "I'll have to resituate her first or I'll smack her head. Jesus, she's been out for a good fifteen minutes. A crack on the nogging might leave her out for hours."

"Come, Mrs. Addison. Take me to your son."

"Wait until we go in first, Doc." Dirk instructs.

"Every second counts when someone is unconscious, Dirk. I'll be fine."

Drake lowers her to the ground before slapping her cheeks with too much force. "Come on, girl. Wake up!"

Letting her head loll around, she moans softly while wishing she could knock the son-of-a-bitch on his ass.

"What a wimp. She certainly won't last much longer." Drake clucks his tongue. "Didn't Walter mention she was an addict?"

"Shut up, Drake. Just carry her inside. I don't like the idea of Doc being inside alone. Something's wrong."

Drake hoists her into his arms, following Dirk. "Thank God, a cot to set her on. Girl's heavy for such a skinny thing."

Seconds after the words leave Drake's mouth, they are followed by two, heavy *thumps*. Drake crumpled to the ground, right next Dirk, but she was ready. She tucks and rolls away.

Wasting no time, Jesse and Jane disarm the men while Lamar ties them up.

"What's going on here?" Dr. Berning asks.

"Securing a way out of this nightmare, that's what." Jesse crosses the cave floor, rifle pointed at the man's head. "Your flight outta here just got delayed. We'll take off when the rest of our group returns."

"How did you know?"

Sensing he is about to faint; she motions toward the cot behind him. "Have a seat, doctor. Can't have the man who's gonna find a cure to this mess damage brain cells. Doesn't matter how we heard. What's important is that we know. We didn't make it this long just to die in a cave from radiation."

"Did you kill them?" Dr. Berning looks behind her toward Drake and Dirk.

"No, they're just taking a good nap." Lamar grins, clearly pleased with the results of the plan. "Their heads will hurt like crazy when they wake up, but they'll be no worse for the wear. We aren't monsters. We're just trying to live."

"Aren't we all?" Dr. Berning's lips tremble. "Seems our chances exponentially dip with each passing day. How long do you plan to wait for the others in your group to return?"

"As long as it takes, so sit tight." Turner tries to sound stern. "We all go, or no one does."

"They'll never agree to taking you with us."

Jesse's anger spikes. "We don't plan on giving them a choice. Either we go with, or you don't. I doubt they'll want to risk losing you."

"There won't be enough room. The plane only seats twelve. These are good people, but they won't hesitate to kill you if necessary. It's nothing personal, I assure you. It's all about survival now."

"Yes, it's all about survival now, Doctor." Turner's cheek flame red, matching his anger. "And like Jesse said, we don't plan on sitting here, waiting to slowly die. If there's a chance to escape somewhere safe, we're taking it."

Jesse senses Dr. Berning is a good man. There is a kind spirit behind the wounded eyes. Setting the rifle down, she walks over and kneels in front of him. "We aren't bad people, either. We aren't. We're all each other has left in this whole, messed up world. All of us have seen things, lost loved ones, had our hearts and souls crushed, during the last week. Before this happened, I was just a girl learning to live life clean and sober, enjoying the company of my boyfriend, working at Walmart, and doing my best to make up for past mistakes to the people I hurt with my addiction. That's changed now, just as I'm sure your world changed.

Everything we know, everything we believe, our complete way of life—it's gone. Brave, wonderful men we love left yesterday to get more supplies so we can live longer. Unfortunately, they left before finding out the news about the radiation. When they return, they'll be devastated to learn they risked their lives for nothing. So, the plan in place is to give them some new hope in the form of getting outta here. Watching my mom blow her head off was horrible, yet somehow, I imagine watching these wonderful people here die slow, painful deaths from radiation poisoning will be even worse."

Tears fill Dr. Berning's kind eyes. "Yes, it's an awful way to die."

"Then please, help us convince them to take us, too. You don't seem like the kind of man who could walk away, knowing you sentenced us to death."

"I'm not, but again, it's simply a matter of logistics. The plane won't hold all of us."

"Can't, or won't?" Turner asks.

"What do you mean?"

"Is twelve the FAA recommended seating, or the actual capacity of the plane? It's not like the pilot will be in trouble for breaking FAA standards."

"I don't know. That's something you'll have to ask the pilot."

"Here's another question—where are y'all heading?" Jane inquires.

"We don't know quite yet. We've got to go somewhere far away from a reactor."

"You're lying!" Lamar steps closer.

"I'm not, I assure you. I may be a scientist, but I don't recall every location of nuclear plants around the world. We must get the map first."

"What map?" Jesse raises an inquisitive brow.

"There's one at the estate of the man who set up the lab. In his library."

"Where?" Jesse senses he is telling the truth.

"Down near Clinton."

Rising to her feet, she looks at the remainder of the group. A new plan rolls around inside her mind. "Then we'll just go get that map. With you, and the directions, in our hands, the negotiations will go our way. Guaranteed."

"That's too risky!" Turner blurts out. "You can't go alone with him! What if he's lying?"

"I'll go." Jane takes a deep breath. "Lamar and Martha can stay here and guard those men. Clinton isn't too far. We'll make it back by midnight."

"Are you both insane?" Lamar appears on the verge of hysterics. "Jesse, there's no way. Too risky! No telling what kind of troubles await y'all out there."

"Lamar, we aren't going to stop. It's not like this is a supply run. We'll drive straight there then come right back. If the place has a library, it's probably expensive. Am I right, Dr. Berning?"

"Yes. And surrounded by a brick wall about fifteen feet high. We locked it up before leaving, so the chances of running into the dead inside are slim. The same can't be said about the roads leading in and out, but the estate is far up in the mountains, and the closest neighbors are at least five miles away."

"Then it's settled. Before Uncle Reed and the others return, we do this. Get back here as soon as possible, tell them of the plan. Have all our ducks in a row, then we'll all head back to your lab, Dr. Berning. If we want to get out of this place alive, we need to stack the deck. Let's roll."

For a few seconds, she worries one—or all—of them will put up an argument.

She's greeted by silence.

All of them, except for Dr. Berning and the two soldiers tied up and out cold by the front door, seem to accept the plan is the best course of action to take. She grabs a rifle and flashlight. Jane does the same.

Turning to face Dr. Berning, she motions for Lamar to tie his hands. "No offense. Just being safe."

"You needn't worry about me. I'm a scientist, not a soldier. Besides, either way this works out, we'll have the map, which is crucial to our survival. Doesn't really matter to me who takes me to get it if they're armed."

"Well said, Doctor." She hugs Turner, Martha, and Lamar, whispering her love before pulling away. Martha hands her a set of keys to one of the Humvees. "We'll be back soon. Lamar, keep an eye on those men. Don't you dare fall asleep."

"On it!" Lamar sets his jaw tight.

Without another word, Jesse leads the trio topside, flicking on the flashlight. She jogs at a brisk pace, hating the sensation of being outside, in the dark, as they run.

We can do this. We have to do this. We will do this. We will continue on.

Chapter 13 - Alternate Route

"SHOULD WE SAY something?"

Cooper tamps down the last pile of dirt over Walter's grave with his boot. "I've already said the Lord's Prayer inside my head, Mason. One don't need to speak for words to be heard."

"Did you know them, I mean, like, were you all friends or just neighbors?"

"I've known Walter for years. Yeah, we were friends. He was a good man. A damn good man. Reed and I went to high school together, but we lost touch when he moved away after graduation. He came back two years ago, but we only had the chance to catch up a few times. He was a good man, too."

"I still can't believe this. We drive hundreds of miles without seeing any signs of life and then run into people you know. Unreal. Good thing I smoke, and the window was down, or we wouldn't have heard the shots, or Kyle yell."

"I would have. I'd recognize his voice anywhere. He's been on the force for years. Kyle's my best officer. Come on, let's go find out what they're doing way up here."

"It was nice of you to be the one to bury Walter and Reed. I think Kyle's done for the day. He looks rough."

Wiping his dirty hands on his pants, Cooper turns around. noting Kyle hasn't moved from the blood-soaked ground next to where Walter and Reed died. Kyle just stares at the pavement, obviously overwhelmed by the events, and the fact he shot Walter. Cooper recognizes the look—utter devastation. He'd felt the same thing only days before in Colorado.

"Guess I've put off long enough talking to him. Best go hear what he has to say."

Mason hands him back the gun and follows. Cooper nods his thanks, surprised the kid stood outside with him while he buried the dead. Then again, Mason surprised him by jumping out of the SUV with Teresa's gun, shooting at the zombies while running. He doubts the moment of heroics was to impress Teresa. Mason is tougher than he previously assumed.

"You afraid he's got bad news about your hometown?" Mason asks.

Nodding, unwilling to say yes out loud because deep down in his heart, the place inside a man's soul rarely visited, he already knows what he is about to hear, yet as long as no one else verbalizes them, they aren't reality. He decides to add a few more minutes to what he senses will be a heartbreaking conversation with Kyle by talking to Mason.

"Mason? You steer clear of Teresa." He stops, using the visual aide of all the dead bodies to bring the point home. "I mean it. She's only out for herself, and that certainly didn't start when the world ended. Women like her are the kind who use men to get what they want. Back in the old world, she'd use her charms and looks to snag a rich man. Now, she'll use them to keep herself alive. If you get tangled up with the likes of her, you'll end up just like those corpses."

"You're wrong, Cooper. She's just—"

"I'm not wrong, son. Want to know what she was thinking while you were passed smooth out on the highway? She was trying to convince me to pass the time away by screwing her, that's what. Of course, her little act wasn't because she wanted me. She wanted what I had, which was the key to the SUV. She said we should just fill the tank with the remaining gas and leave you behind. That's the kind of woman she is. Cold.

Callous. Willing to do or say anything to get what she wants."

The look of shock on Mason's face makes him feel bad for hurting his feelings, but it cannot be helped. The boy needs to be aware, and if he still opts to pursue the woman, Cooper won't feel guilty if things turn out bad.

"That bitch!" Mason looks toward their SUV. "You promise you aren't bullshitting me? You don't have eyes for her, do you?"

Despite the horrors of the last two hours, and the fact he knows he is about to find out news no father ever wants to hear, he laughs. "Son, she could be the last snatch on earth, and I'd still walk away. My Johnson would rather die lonely of old age than get shredded to pieces."

"If you don't trust her, then why in the world did you let her come this far with us?"

"Because that's just who I am. Besides, we needed an extra set of eyes on the road. Now, I'm done talking about her. Let's go check on Kyle."

Dodging the dead on the ground, they walk across the parking lot. Kyle doesn't flinch or give any indication he hears them approach.

"Kyle? Come on, get up. It'll be dark soon. It ain't safe outside."

"It ain't safe anywhere, Chief."

Steadying himself, he asks the question burning a hole inside his heart. "What were y'all doing up this far north?"

Kyle gazes up, and the look on his face makes Cooper's heart clench.

"Because we had no choice, Chief. Malvern's gone. What the dead didn't destroy, the government did."

"Oh, shit!" Mason gasps. "All of it?"

Kyle rises, readjusting his rifle. "Yes. Only a few of us escaped. Walt took us to a cave near Blanchard Springs, and we've been holed up there ever since."

Cooper forces the words out. "My children? Did you see—?"

"We tried to save them, Chief. We hunkered down inside Walmart. Charlie and Charlene were there, but when the soldiers attacked us, everyone panicked and scattered. I'm sorry, sir, but they didn't make it out of the parking lot."

He tries holding back the tears, remain strong and tough, suck up the crushing sorrow, but fails. Sobs of anguish fill the quiet parking lot. "All this way…I made it all this way…for nothing!"

"That's not true, Cooper. You saved me, Teresa, and Kyle. You're a hero in my book. God, I'm so sorry, but please, don't give up now." Mason's tone is soft, comforting. "We need you. I need you."

"So do I, Chief. Martha Addison's gonna kill me when I tell her I let Walt die, if Jane Richmond doesn't get to me first. Jesus H. Christ! I can't believe this shit!" Kyle kicks the back tire on the nearest Humvee.

The sound of feet running causes them to turn their heads. Cooper and Kyle raise their weapons.

"More coming this way! Run!" Teresa screams.

Looking behind her, Cooper sees a handful of the dead less than twenty yards behind Teresa.

"Humvee! Now!" Kyle orders.

All three men jump inside the vehicle, Kyle behind the wheel. Mason holds the back door open, screaming for Teresa to hurry.

"Start, you piece of government shit!" Kyle pounds the dashboard.

"Hurry, Kyle. They're closing in fast!" Cooper urges.

Teresa bursts inside and Mason slams the door. The engine coughs and sputters before starting.

"Hang on!" Kyle yells.

Several of the creatures ram their dead bodies into the side doors.

Kyle guns the engine. The Humvee bounces over the corpses like they are nothing more than burnt speed bumps. Tires bark as he turns onto the highway. Cooper watches the mangled, deformed bodies fade into the distance.

For the next several miles, no one speaks. Kyle finally slows down after the road grows curvier.

"Looks like you got a lot of supplies." Teresa comments while poking through the boxes in the back.

"Which I'd gladly trade for the lives of my friends." Kyle's tone is harsh. "We've got people to deliver them to, so hands off until we get back to the cave."

"Cave? Are you kidding me? You're taking us to a cave? That's your safe house?" Teresa whines.

"Yeah, I am, unless you want me to drop you off at one of these empty homes along the way? Let you have free housing, senorita?"

"Okay, let's all take a minute to breathe here." Cooper intervenes. "Let the adrenaline rush wane."

"Easier said than done, Chief. Been living off an adrenaline high ever since this mess started! God, this is the second trip to the store that cost me people I care about. And, it seems, human munchers ain't our only enemies. Walt was right about animals, and he didn't even know it."

Cooper swallows hard. "Yeah, I thought my eyes were playing tricks on me. They looked like hellhounds. You said second trip. What did you mean?"

"I mean I lost the woman I love in the first one, and two great friends today. All because of fucking drugs!"

"Regina's gone, too?" Cooper gasps.

Kyle bites his lip for several seconds before responding. "Yep. She saved our lives by giving up hers."

"You mentioned drugs. Is that what caused all this?"

"Yeah, Chief. Want to know why we're in this mess? Brace yourselves—it's insane."

For the past two hours, Cooper, Mason, and Teresa sat in stunned silence while Kyle talked nonstop. By the time he finished, his mind cannot take any more.

It is all over. No hope left and nothing for him to keep on living for because his wife and children are dead. His hometown was destroyed. There isn't a single reason to keep fighting, keep struggling, while watching the few remaining people he knows die as well.

He'd wait to end it all until Mason is safe with the others before heading out into the woods and putting a bullet into his brain. Join his wife and children on the other side rather than roaming around in an undead shell, eating other survivors.

"Kyle, how far do we have before arriving?" Mason breaks the deafening silence.

"About five minutes. Then, we'll hike for another few miles."

"Joy." Teresa rolls her eyes.

Kyle stiffens. "Hey, I can always stop, remember? There's plenty of illegals in this part of the state. Maybe you'll run into one of your relatives. Shack up with them instead of us gringos. I'm not in the mood to listen to a whiny, bitchy woman, so if you want to keep riding with us, shut the fuck up."

Turning his head, Cooper stares out the window, a smile tugging at the corner of his lips. Yep, Officer Kyle Pender was the best man on the force, able to sniff out trouble in seconds, and he pegged Teresa as a problem right from the start.

Wish I'd done the same thing. No, I wish I was still next to Karla's warm body, dreaming. God, this just can't be how the world ends.

Can it?

***

Teresa feels sick to her stomach, and it isn't just from barely escaping from the dead again.

Listening to the words from the lips of the obnoxious bastard named Kyle made her heart pound. For the first time since she woke up inside the basement of her home in Phoenix, everything made sense. Sick, twisted, out-of-this-world sense.

While Cooper drove toward Arkansas after rescuing the stupid kid, Teresa occupied her time by reading more from Roberto's journal. The words confused her, most written in a combination of phrases and drug dealer lingo she wasn't entirely familiar with, yet what she gleaned from the pages was a new batch had been created, a big shipment was coming, and Benito seemed to have made some sort of pact with other drug cartels.

Now, everything is crystal clear. She doesn't know anything about science or chemical formulas or how drugs are distributed, but she knows enough. She understands how Maria turned and why Roberto fled without her, and most importantly, why the world collapsed so fast.

Drugs are everywhere. People from all walks of life indulge, and their addiction is what kept Louboutin's on her feet, Dior and Chanel inside her closet, and what paid for the sprawling, six-million-dollar mansion in Phoenix.

And the one in El Salvador.

There is no doubt how the nightmare started, and where.

She's got to figure out a way to get back to El Salvador. To do that, she must keep her mouth shut and not anger the rednecks or she'll end up on foot. Once they get to the cave, she'll wait until everyone falls asleep, slit Kyle's throat, take the keys to this Humvee, and head toward the coast. She'll do whatever is necessary to find someone with a boat. Surely the dead corpses can't swim. Her mission now is to get to El Salvador, find Benito, and then cut pieces of flesh from his bones and feed them to the dead.

While he watches.

Whatever it takes, she's going home.

They pull into what looks like a campground. Another Humvee sits by a trail leading into the dark forest. She hates the outdoors but keeps her opinions to herself.

"Shit."

"What's wrong, Kyle?" Cooper asks.

"One of the Humvee's is missing. We only took two."

Cooper's hand immediately finds the butt of the pistol in his waistband. "Maybe one of the others took it and went searching for supplies like ya'll did?"

"No way." Kyle shakes his head. "Turner broke his leg and can't walk. Martha would never leave his side, and I doubt Jesse would, either. That leaves Jane Richmond or Lamar Wilson. The only reason either of them would leave is either Turner's taken a turn for the worse, or someone else got hurt—bad enough Jane can't patch them up. No talking and keep your eyes and ears open. Hurry!"

Everyone jumps out and follows Kyle up the trail.

"Ladies' first." Cooper points at Teresa.

Sighing, she falls into step behind Kyle.

"Jesse, turn left here. We go about six miles. The road ends at the driveway."

"Gotcha, Doc."

"God, I can't believe you just ran them down. I'm so glad you're driving." Jane's voice is taut with fear. "I'da freaked out and probably crashed into a tree or something. How many was that last one, Doc? Eight?"

"Twelve. I agree with your friend back there, Jesse. You're driving skills are quite impressive. Did you aspire being a race car driver?"

Jesse's laughter is tinged with bitterness. "Better them than us. And no, my mom taught me. She was a cop."

"She did a fine job."

"Regina was an amazing woman." Jane adds. Everett hears the heavy sadness in her voice. "If it weren't for her sacrifice, Jesse and I wouldn't still be alive."

"Not now, Jane, I don't want to think about my—oh, shit!"

Everett's head slams into the passenger window. The Humvee spins. Jane screams from the backseat.

"God, they're everywhere!" Jesse yells. "Hang on!"

His bound hands cling to the seat while forcing the bile burning in his throat back down. Now is not the time to have a bout with car sickness. A corpse bounces off the hood and into the windshield. Thankfully, the glass doesn't break, but it is full of small, spider-web looking cracks.

Bam!

His attempts to keep from vomiting fail. The bloody creature's face smashes against the glass, leaving chunks of flesh behind. Bending over, he pukes all over the floorboard.

"Jesse! To your right! Look out!" Jane screams.

"Hang on to that rifle, Jane! Doctor, can you use a weapon?"

"I'm familiar, yes. Any good? Afraid not."

"You best figure it out, because if I can't get past them, we're gonna need all the firepower we got! Jane? Untie him."

The engine roars and rumbles as Jesse pushes it to the limit, driving through the mass of corpses, running into them as though they are sacks of mud. Jane reaches over the seat and cuts the rope binding his wrists.

She racks the slide before handing him a pistol. "Don't you miss, you hear me? Don't you miss!"

"You said there's a fence surrounding this place? Gated?" Jesse queries.

"Yes. We aren't far. Maybe half a mile?"

Thump. Thump. Thump.

"Metal?"

"Yes."

"Then we're just gonna drive through that shit like it ain't even there. Can we get inside, Doc? You said it was locked."

"Break a fucking window!" Jane's voice is on the verge of hysterical.

"There! I see it!" Jesse pushes her foot all the way down on the accelerator. The Humvee groans in protest.

Looking behind them, Everett notices they put distance between the vehicle and the undead. He does a few mental calculations, and the results cause his stomach to lurch again.

"We've got maybe two minutes from the time we pull up if you maintain this current rate of speed."

"I'm sure not slowing down." Jesse glances in the rearview mirror. "If that's all the time we've got, then you better run like hell the second we stop."

"What...what are you saying?" Everett stutters.

"I'm saying we'll pull up, you go in, get that fucking map, and run back outside. If any of those things beat your estimated timetable, we'll shoot them. Give you a chance to make it back in one piece."

His mouth gapes open. "I…no way. I can't run. Old injury."

"No excuses, just do it! Grab something and hold on, folks. I'm going through the gate!"

The impact of hitting the thick wrought iron makes the Humvee shudder. The grating sound of metal on metal hurts his ears. A weird, grinding noise fills the cab as Jesse maneuvers the vehicle up to the front door.

"What's that sound?" Jane asks.

The engine shudders and dies.

Jesse tries restarting it, but nothing happens.

"Inside! Now!" Everett yells. "Follow me!"

The three jump out of the Humvee and run to the big, bay window by the front door. Jesse pushes him aside. "Move!"

She fires into the glass. A section the size of a bowling ball shatters. Leaning back, she raises her foot and kicks the shards until making a hole big enough for them to climb through.

"God, they're close! I can hear them." Jane whines.

Everett moves as fast as his old legs let him. He is breathing so hard he fears a heart attack is only seconds away. "Come on. The library doesn't have any windows, and the doors are solid oak. There's a trap door in the floor that leads to the garage. Hurry!"

"What kind of man lived here?" Jesse asks, inches behind Everett.

"The smartest man I've ever known. Here, through this door."

The trio scrambled inside the room, he slams the door shut, turns the deadbolt, and backs away. "I need a flashlight, please."

Jesse holds one out. "Hurry up, then turn it off. We've got to stay quiet, or they'll hear us."

Flicking the light on, he heads straight to the shelf he remembers the book was on. Sure enough, it rests in the same place. *History of Nuclear Power* by James A. Mahaffey. He's never been so glad to see a book in his entire life.

"Shit! Did you hear that? Turn the light off!" Jesse whispers from behind him. "They're here."

Everett complies, and the three huddle together near the bookcase.

Warm breath grazes his ear. "Doc, where's the trap door?"

"Follow me."

Dropping down to all fours, feeling around in the dark for the large desk in the middle of the room, he finds it after bumping his head. Latching his fingers onto the edge of the Persian rug, he pulls it back. The sounds of the dead outside make him work faster. It takes a few more seconds to find the latch and open the door. Sticking his arm down as far as it will go, he turns on the flashlight. Thankfully, nothing is inside the tunnel except cobwebs and dirt.

"Be careful climbing down." He guides Jane's hand to the opening.

The sound of breaking glass sends all of them into panic mode.

Jane loses her grip and tumbles down the hole. Her yelp of pain makes his heart pound.

Jesse is next, followed by Everett. As he lowers the trap door, the sounds of growling and mumbling from the hallway make the hair stand erect all over his body. He secures the latch, hoping the corpses haven't figured out how to open doors.

"Jane? Are you okay?" Jesse asks.

"Didn't break anything, just sprained my ankle."

"Can you walk?"

"Yes, just slowly."

Jesse sighs. "How far to the garage, Dr. Berning?"

"Two hundred yards, tops. Maybe we should wait here a few minutes and allow Jane to rest and give the creatures a chance to gather inside the house so we can slip out back to the Humvee?"

"Why, so we can sit there and pray for it to start?"

"Sorry. I'm old, and I'm not thinking straight, Jesse. This was my first encounter."

"You just broke your cherry, old man. No fun, is it?"

"Not at all. So, what's the plan, Jesse? Wait here until the others arrive? You know they'll come looking if we don't return."

"Fuck no. This is way worse than being inside the cave. This is like being trapped inside one long casket. Any vehicles inside the garage? Keys?"

Everett smiles, a genuine smile, for the first time in days. "There's another Humvee. Dr. Thomas loved the thing. The keys are on the garage wall, at least, they were when we left."

"Information we needed like ten minutes ago!" Jesse throws her hands in the air. "Go, lead the way. We gotta get out of here before I lose it. This is too close for comfort for me."

"You'll do just fine, dear. I don't doubt that one bit. We'll need to walk, though. My legs are about give out and Jane can't run."

"Long strides, Doctor. Long strides. I'll help Jane. God, I can't believe I'm about to say this, but I want to go back to the cave."

"Me, too. There's probably a ton of spiders in here. God, I hate spiders!" Jane mumbles from behind them as Jesse helps her stand.

"I do, too, but not as much as those corpses above us. Let's go!"

"How long does it take to give some stupid kid medicine? Wake him up from nappy-time? They should be back by now."

"I agree, Warton, which is a first for me. Something's wrong."

"Gee, Clive, glad my thoughts get your seal of approval."

"Shut up! Both of you!" Denaryl yells. "Warton, is there an off switch on your mouth?"

"Only when it's eating, licking, or sleeping." Kevin chortles. "I'm serious, though. We need to go check on them. My gut's on fire."

"Yeah, mine too." Denaryl stares at the monitors. "I can't see shit except black forest. They could've got ambushed. The dead pilots may have bitten others."

Kevin shakes his head. "Maybe, but I suspect the little visit by those two broads was staged."

"That's crazy." Clive rolls his eyes. "Kevin, do you really think an old woman and young girl would risk their lives and trek through those dangerous woods alone?"

"Don't you? Age doesn't matter when it comes to dark intentions."

Denaryl checks his rifle. "As much as I hate to admit it, Warton's right. Something is wrong, and our brothers are out there. So is Dr. Berning. Our number one priority is keeping him safe. We let our guard down earlier, but I say we make up for that mistake now. If we're wrong, no harm's been done. If we're right, well, then we do what we do best. Winters? Just in case things go sour, go get the bag with Dr. Berning's notes. We might not get the opportunity to come back if we run into trouble. Warton? Get the keys to the truck."

"Thank God! A real mission. Anything's better than being trapped here." Clive jumps to his feet.

Ten minutes later, the men leave the control room and head topside.

"This is the first time we've all worked as a real group while agreeing on our objective." Kevin laughs. "Just like old times, eh Clive?"

"Except this time, our enemies are corpses, but okay, I get the analogy."

Denaryl snaps his fingers to command their attention. "Focus, you two. If our suspicions are correct, shoot to kill. No questions, no explanations. Bury those civvies."

Not another word is spoken as they stop out into the night. They pull down their night vision goggles and enter the woods on silent feet, adrenaline high and senses heightened.

Twenty minutes later, Denaryl holds up a hand. The all stop and listen. Footsteps from about fifty yards away crunch through the dry leaves. Faint beams from a flashlight dance through the woods.

Four separate strides, no doubt, and they are coming up the trail.

Fast.

Denaryl gives the signal. The trio fan out, heading to intercept the intruders.

Chapter 14 - A United Front

"STOP PACING, MOM. You'll just tire yourself out. They'll be back soon."

"I can't sit still. Feels like I'm about to jump outta my skin. I hate waiting!"

Turner chuckles softly. "Yeah, patience was never one of your virtues."

The look on his mother's face reminds him of all the times he'd said the wrong thing as a kid. Just like his father, he feared no other person on the planet except his mother.

"You realize this is an exercise in futility, right? Our friends will come looking for us, and when they get here, they won't play nice."

Lamara stiffens. "I don't believe anyone was talking to you, grunt."

"Dirk. My name's Dirk Kincannon. You got cotton in your head, old man? How many times do I have to tell you we aren't military?"

"Once a government tool, always a government tool." Turner replies.

"Does your father fall into that category, too?"

"You shut your mouth! My husband retired with honors, and he regrets every minute he was under their control!"

"So do we, ma'am. Trust me. That's why we left." Dirk clears his throat. "We aren't animals, you know."

"Maybe not, but you aren't quite human, either. Ya'll were just gonna leave us here and let us die without even warning us what was coming! That's cold-blooded reptile behavior in my book."

"There's not enough room for all of us! It's not personal. We've had to make some hard choices during the last few days. This was one of them."

"Denton, right?" Lamar asks the other man who spoke.

"Yeah. Drake Denton."

"Okay, Drake? If you want to take another nap, then continue running your trap."

"Let's tone things back a little. Sound reverberates here. All this yelling gave me a headache."

"Mom, please, sit down." Turner softens his tone. "Everybody will be back soon, and then we can get the hell outta here."

"We can't take you with us, I'm sorry. Though a brilliant plan you had here, there simply isn't room."

His mother sets her jaw while glaring at Dirk. "Then we'll make room, Mr. Kincannon. The choice is simple: your pilot makes two runs, the first with our group and your doctor, and the second for the rest of you."

"Pardon me for being rude, Mrs. Addison, but are you crazy? You really don't think we'll agree to that, do you?"

"If you want to keep your precious doctor alive, you will."

"What are you going to do if he doesn't make it back? What happens if they die out there? Then where will your leverage be? I'll tell you—dead."

"That's enough!" Lamar roars, rising from his perch on the cot. "I know what you two are doing. Trying to whip us into a frenzy, make us so angry we lose focus on you—give you a chance to escape. Ain't gonna happen. Be quiet or I'll shut you both up!"

Turner glances over to his mom, afraid she is close to passing out. He doubts she's slept more than three hours in the past two days. Dark circles rim her eyes, and her face is drawn tight. The veins in her neck and temples pulse from a rapid heartbeat. "Mom? Help me move to a different position, please? My back's in a bind."

"Sure thing, baby."

Waiting until she leans down to help and is close enough no one else will hear, he whispers, "Mom? Sit down. Your blood pressure's spiking, isn't it?"

"I'm fine."

"No, you aren't. You really want to pass out, or worse, and leave Lamar as the only one between me and those men?"

The words, spoken with the intention of forcing her to sit down, work. "Okay, but just for a minute."

The sound of gunshots fills the cave.

"Someone's firing outside!" Lamar runs toward the entrance.

"Wait! It could be the other men!" Martha screams.

"Or it could be Walt and them fighting off the dead! Either way, I ain't sitting here waiting to see what comes through that door!"

"Lamar, don't!" Turner yells, but it is too late. Lamar disappears.

His mother picks up two rifles and hands him one while nodding at their captives. "Shoot them if they try to leave."

Turner says a silent prayer while watching his mother disappear into the night.

***

"Mason, no!"

Cooper's heart breaks as the boy's head explodes in front of him. Chunks of Mason's blood and skull splashes across his face.

All touch with reality gone, he loses it, running full force, firing rounds in the direction of the bullet. "He's just a kid! He's just a kid!"

His body jerks to the right when a bullet rips through his shoulder, but he doesn't care. Rage thrums throughout his system, blocking the pain. He continues running, following the flashes from the guns bursting out of the barrels with each round.

He knows he hit a target when a man's voice yells up ahead yells, "Shit!"

"Ready for another one, you bastard? Come on, come on out here and face me like a man! Only pussies hide in the shadows, picking off kids! Come on!"

"Drop your weapons, or we'll take all of you down. The first shot was a warning!"

"You drop yours, asshole, or we'll kill Dr. Berning! Got a gun to his head right now!"

The familiar voice of Martha Addison yelling at a man in the woods makes wonder if he is hallucinating.

"I said drop them! If you want to make that flight, you'll need him, and the map!"

Kyle and Teresa come up behind Cooper and stop. Kyle grabs him by the arm, yanking him to the ground. "That's Martha, but I have no clue what she means."

His skins pickles at the sounds of a scuffle about thirty feet ahead of their position.

"Walt? That you out there?"

"Lamar?" Kyle answers.

"Yeah, we got 'em. Come on up."

Cooper glances back at Mason's body on the trail. "Go ahead. I'll fetch him."

"Let me help." Teresa offers.

"No. My responsibility. You stay with Kyle."

Teresa shakes her head. "No, I'll help. He was a good kid."

"Hang on, Lamar. We'll be right there." Kyle turns his attention back to Cooper. "We can't risk burying him in the dark. Come on, we'll carry him the rest of the way. Tomorrow morning, we'll give him a proper burial."

"Cooper, you're bleeding!" Teresa gasps.

"You take a bullet?" Kyle asks.

Shoulders sagging with grief, he nods once and rises, tears streaming down his face, wishing the bullet that took out Mason would have missed and killed him instead.

***

"Go through that door, nice and easy." Martha's gaze bounces from man to man, making sure they comply. "Try any fancy tricks and I'll blow a hole through your heads. Guaranteed."

"Where's the rest of our group?"

"Keep walking, hands up." Her nerves are on edge while walking behind the two carrying the body of the third who'd taken a bullet. "Set him on that cot, right there, and then back away."

"Rice, what happened to Winters?" Dirk asks from his spot on the floor.

"Took one to thigh. He's bleeding out. Fast. Where's Dr. Berning? We need him!"

"He ain't here, so you best use your field training." Martha nods toward a medical kit near Turner.

"What? You said—"

"I lied." She points the rifle directly at the man named Rice. "Best not waste time worrying about why, just help your friend. Lamar? Get them the first aid kit."

Lamar moves across the cave floor in quick strides, grabs the kit and tosses it to Denaryl.

"You okay, Kincannon? Denton?"

"They're fine, I assure you. We ain't killers like y'all are."

The other man standing next to Rice snorts. "So, the comment about blowing our heads off was a joke, right?"

"Warton!" Dirk snaps. "You and Rice shut up and concentrate on Winters. Right now."

"We just need a ride on your plane." Martha takes a deep breath, hoping it will help calm her down. "Give us what we want, and everybody lives."

"I knew something was wrong." Denaryl grinds his jaw. "I knew it!"

Denaryl and the one named Warton turn their attention to their friend. She backs up several steps toward Turner. "What's taking them so long?"

"Probably had to pick up the supplies they dropped during the ambush." Lamar offers. "They'll be in directly, Ms. Martha."

She doesn't speak while watching the five men in the cave, gaze bouncing between the two tied up on the floor and the three across the room at the last cot. Her heartbeat is erratic, and she feels lightheaded. A weird buzzing noise rings inside her ears. She fears she'll vomiting any second. Turner was right—her blood pressure is sky high.

"Hey! They're back!" Turner yells, drawing her attention to the door. "Thank goodness! Oh, my God! Chief Hollingsworth? Is that you?"

Martha's mouth goes dry when only three people walk inside. She notices Kyle's clothes are covered in dried blood as he makes his way toward her position. Chills scramble up her back at the haunted look on his face. Turner's question—and the answer staring back at her from across the room with a wound to his shoulder—causes her breath to come in short gasps.

"Kyle? Where's my husband? Reed?"

He is right in front of her now, tears running down his dirty face. Kyle doesn't need to say a word. His silence rips a hole through her heart.

She collapses to her knees. "No. God, no!"

"Dad?" Turner whimpers from across the room.

She tries to get up and go to her son, but she lacks the strength to move. The buzzing inside her head increases while she sobs, body trembling. Darkness descends over her mind.

Walter. No. My Walter. What am I going to do without you?

***

"What happened out there?"

Kyle finishes bandaging Cooper's shoulder before answering Turner's question. "Now's not the time for that discussion. Just know your dad died a hero. He saved my life. We'll talk about that later once your mom wakes. I don't want to tell the story more than once because I don't think I can. Okay?"

Tears trickle down Turner's face, making Kyle feel worse. "She's gonna be okay, right?"

"Yes, son. She just fainted. She'll be fine."

"What about Bailey and Allsop?"

He shrugs his shoulders. "Don't know what happened to them, Lamar. They decided to go it alone to get their families."

"Pieces of shit."

"Agree." He motions toward the other men and asks Turner, "Want to tell me why they're here? And where's Jesse and Jane?"

"They went with Dr. Berning to go get a map."

His mouth drops open. "Come again? Did you say a map?"

Though he knows Turner is heartbroken over the loss of his father, something else burns behind his eyes. Something beyond sorrow, or fear, or even terror. It takes him a few seconds to pinpoint the emotion.

Dread. Heavy, soul-crushing dread.

Turner takes a deep breath while glancing over at the other men. "We've got more problems than just the dead on the horizon."

Teresa edges closer, gaze laser-focused on Turner. "What kind of problems?"

"Radiation from the power plant in Russellville. Dr. Berning said a meltdown will happen soon, and then the shit will come this way. His group planned on leaving tomorrow in some plane they have access to and head someplace without a nuclear power plant close by."

Cooper stiffens. "I forgot all about Arkansas Nuclear One! It ain't too far away."

"Map? And why are those fools here, Lamar?" Kyle urges.

"I heard two of them talking in the woods about it the other day. When I came back and spread the news, we decided if they're leaving, so are we. Together. Figured we needed an ace in the hole to make them take us, so Jesse and Martha convinced Dr. Berning to come here and offer medical help to Turner."

"Let me get this straight—the plan was to hold them hostage and force them to take us, yet they left to get a map? What the fuck, Lamar?"

"The doc said their plan was to go get a map that listed all the reactors around the world. That way, they'd know which location to head to that didn't have one. Jesse figured if we had the doctor and the map, they'd have no choice but to let us go with them."

"I know a place where there's not a nuclear power plant." Teresa interrupts.

"Where?" Turner's brows raise in suspicion.

"El Salvador. It's where I'm from."

"That's too far away!" Kyle snaps. "Besides, what the hell are we gonna do once we get there? Go live in the jungle?"

"My father has a big estate about thirty miles from San Salvador. There's room for all of us, I swear. It's surrounded by high walls and basically a fortress."

Ignoring the stupid woman, Kyle addresses Turner. "How long have Jesse and the others been gone? And where were they heading?"

"About three hours. They went to Clinton."

"Sonofabitch! That's a populated area. There's no telling how many munchers!" Kyle jumps to his feet and stomps across the room, stopping directly in front of Dirk Kincannon. "How many does it hold, and who's flying it?"

"The plane holds twelve. Rice is our pilot." Dirk nods toward the large man sitting near the wounded one.

"Is it true? About the radiation? Your plans to evacuate in the morning?"

"Yes."

"Any more of your men left at the lab?"

"No. It's just us and Dr. Berning."

Kyle kneels in front of Dirk. "Look, I won't apologize for what they did to lure you here. I'm sure you understand their fears. We've all been through hell and back, and I found out another terrifying tidbit I ain't shared with them just yet. It will affect us all, no matter where we go."

"And that would be?"

"It ain't just humans affected by this. A pack of reanimated dead dogs took down one of the men in my group."

"Holy shit." Dirk's eyes nearly bulge out of their sockets.

"Please, I'm begging you. We've got a total of thirteen, counting us all. I can tell you're a man of your word. Agree to take us with you, and we'll all work as a team. That map must be of great importance my friends decided to risk their lives to get it. They ain't back yet, which means they probably ran into trouble. We'll need to pack up what we can and carry the wounded to the Humvees. You have my word my group will work with you and yours. I ain't got anyone's life to swear on anymore, but I promise, if you help us, we'll do the same."

Dirk gives a slight nod. "Agreed."

Kyle rises and addresses the room. "Looks like we're heading out. We'll all be working as one unit now. They've agreed to let us come with them if we agree to stand and fight by their sides. Can ya'll do that? Work as a team, put the past behind us, and find a safe place to live out our future? Only aim at the dead, and not at each other?"

"If it means getting out of this cave alive, hell yeah." Turner nods.

"Anyone got something to say? Now's the time."

No one does.

Kyle bends over and removes the ropes from Dirk and Drake. "Don't make me regret this. I'm putting a lot of lives in your hands. If this goes sour, I swear, I'll come back and eat your faces off."

"I gave you my word, Kyle. I don't go back on it." Dirk rubs his wrists. "Now, let's get to packing. Drake, you, and Warton, fix those cots into gurneys to carry out Winters and Turner. Tell Denaryl to come here and help us secure food. We leave in thirty."

Cooper walks toward the cave's entrance. "I can't leave without taking care of Mason first and could use some help digging a grave."

"I'll help you, Cooper." Teresa joins him. "Like you said, he was a good kid, and he deserves a final resting place."

Kyle looks at his former chief and can tell he won't budge on the idea. He'd been insistent to bury Reed and Walter back in Bentonville, too, despite the dangers of remaining out in the open. "There're tools by the front door. Hurry and be careful."

***

"There's no gas in the tank. Shit!"

"There's a pump right over—oh, sorry, Jesse. I forgot there's no power."

"It's okay, Dr. Berning. We're all scatterbrained."

"Okay, let's think about this." Jane sighs. "We've been gone for what, four hours now?"

Dr. Berning glances at his watch. "Five."

"They'll come looking for us. I know it. I say we just wait here."

"And I'm sure the others at the lab didn't like us being gone for so long. I imagine they're looking for me."

Jesse stiffens. "Do they know where our camp is?"

"Yes. Kevin Warton followed Mr. Addison the first day they met."

"Oh, shit! Will they—"

"Use deadly force? Yes, if they feel threatened. They are former soldiers, you know."

"Then we aren't gonna just sit here and wait! There's got to be some gas around here or a way to get it from the pump. Jane? Hand me the flashlight, please."

She makes a loop in the garage, searching every crook and crevice for signs of a gas can.

"Look! There's one!" Racing over, she picks it up. "And it's full!"

"Hallelujah!" Jane claps her hands.

Running back to the Humvee, Jesse hefts the can and fills the tank.

"I'll get the keys." Dr. Berning limps across the concrete floor. "That's two problems solved, and just leaves one."

"Which is?" She drops the empty can on the ground.

"The door."

"What?"

"The door. Which one of us is going to open it? Jane nor I can run."

"Then I will. Jane, you get behind the wheel. Doc, you get in the passenger seat and roll down the window, rifle ready. Aim for their heads, not the body."

"I'm not a very good shot, Jesse."

"Tonight, you will be, or this is the end of the road for us. Leave the back door open. I'll be in a big hurry to get inside once I do this. Jane—the second I'm in—you slam the pedal to the floor."

"Okay, but as soon as we can, we'll need to switch places." Jane's face is deathly white. "I don't think I can handle smashing into them like you did."

"You can do it, Jane. I know you can. Start her up."

Jane climbs into the driver's seat while Dr. Berning settles in on the passenger side. Jesse walks over to the garage door, hand hovering above the latch until Jane starts the engine.

"One; two; three!" The sound of the metal door opening is loud. She doesn't look out into the yard, afraid of what she may see. Instead, she runs back to the Humvee and jumps inside. "Go!"

Jane floors it. The Humvee shoots out of the garage. The bright headlights and noise caught the attention of the dead roaming around the front yard. Jane screams yet keeps driving.

"Just follow the road, Jane. Don't veer from it! You're doing just fine!"

The ride is bumpy and rough, yet Jane manages to keep the Humvee steady, mashing bodies as she drives. By the time they reach the main road, they are clear.

Jesse pats Jane's shoulder. "See there? I knew you could do it! Uncle Reed's gonna be so proud of you!"

"Yes, fine job, Jane. Fine job." Dr. Berning wipes sweat from his brow. "That was some ride! At least this time, I didn't throw up."

Jane's arms tremble. "Crap, my adrenaline's crashing fast. We need to switch places."

After Jane pull over onto the shoulder, the women swap seats. Jesse puts the Humvee in drive and eases back onto the highway.

"Are my eyes playing tricks on me, or are those headlights?" Dr. Berning squints through the windshield.

"Jesus, let's hope they ain't soldiers!" Jesse grips the wheel harder.

"They're flashing their lights at us! I bet it's Reed and Walter. I knew they'd come looking for us!" Jane squeals.

"Don't be so sure, Jane. Could be a ploy to get us to stop. I see two sets of headlights which don't make sense. They wouldn't risk taking two. Gotta be soldiers." A knot of fear rumbles inside her stomach. They've gone through too much, come way too far, to let the quest end at the hands of more government goons. "Dr. Berning, be ready with that rifle. I mean it."

The two Humvees barrel down the highway. Jesse slows to a stop in the middle of the road and rolls down the window. "Give me a rifle, Jane. Take the wheel if I floor it. I'll be busy shooting."

The first Humvee pulls within ten feet.

"Jesse? It's Kyle!"

"Thank God!" she yells back. "Yeah, it's us!"

Handing the rifle back to Jane, she pulls up alongside Kyle's Humvee. She's never been so glad to see a friendly face.

"We're heading to the hangar, so follow us!" Kyle nods to the right. "We've got everyone, and they've agreed to let us go with them. You got the map?"

"Best news I've heard since all this happened! Yes, we got it. Let's get outta here!"

The two Humvees pull forward, waiting for Jesse to turn hers around and follow. Once the convoy is moving, she smiles while looking over at the doctor, who seems shocked by the turn of events.

"Well, how about that, Dr. Berning? Guess the power of persuasion just made us travel buddies. Between my uncle and Turner's dad, they convinced them to take us. What a Christmas present!"

He looks down at his watch and then out the window. "It's after midnight. Christmas is officially over."

She ignores the weird comment, busying herself with driving and talking with Jane. Knowing their world is about to change—this time for the better—is the best high she's ever experienced.

Ever.

Chapter 15 - Crushing Blows
Friday, December 26th – 1:15 a.m. – Central Standard
Time

DIRK PULLS INTO the parking lot of the small airport near Clinton, does a full circle of the area so the headlights can illuminate any potential threats. Seeing nothing, he drives over to the first hangar where the Gulfstream is housed.

"Please, don't say anything to them. Let me tell Jane. Turner will tell Jesse." Martha requests from the back seat.

"Of course. Let us go inside first and perform a thorough sweep to make sure we're alone. Then, while we prep the plane, you can have some private time."

"Thank you, Mr. Kincannon." Martha whispers, voice thick with emotion. "For everything."

"Welcome, ma'am. Okay, Warton, you ready?"

"On it." Kevin nods. "Be back in two shakes."

Dirk stops directly in front of the door. Kevin jumps out, rifle ready, and dashes inside. Not a sound is made by any of the occupants of the Humvee while they wait for him to return.

Kevin appeared back at the door, thumbs up.

"All clear! Let's go!" Dirk lets out a long breath.

In seconds, all three Humvees are inside the large area and Kevin shuts the door.

"Mrs. Addison, let's get you and Turner inside the plane first and then we'll bring in Jane and Jesse."

"Martha. After all this, please, call me Martha."

Dirk nods. "Drake? I need some help with Turner."

The men climb out and open the back door. They ease the injured kid from the backseat, Martha right behind them. Kevin moves ahead and prepares the plane's stairs as a young woman runs toward them.

He notices Martha stiffens. "Jesse, get Jane over here, please. We'll need some help situating Turner in a seat."

The strength in the woman's voice, the sheer determination not to give any indication something is wrong, causes him to shake his head. His initial perception of Martha as an overwrought, unstable woman he'd met in the woods, vanishes.

"God, losing her uncle is just gonna destroy her."

"Martha, she has you and your son to lean on. Did you see all the gore on the Humvee? Their drive here wasn't an easy one. She's tough."

Not another word is spoken while Dirk and Drake take the stairs. Kevin had already turned the cabin lights on, so they made their way to the back row of seats and set Turner down in the aisle.

"Okay, let's load her up with the supplies. Warton, where's Dee?"

"Already in the cockpit doing his preflight check."

"Find Doc and get the map."

"Baby, we did it. We got the map. Oh, you should've seen Jane! She ran right over those corpses like a champ!"

Dirk steps out of the way as Jesse rushes past him, Martha, and Jane, a few steps behind. "He's all set, ladies. Excuse us while we get things loaded up. Should take about a half-hour."

"Thank you for taking us. Means the world to us all." Jane gushes.

Dirk forces a smile and doesn't reply as he and Drake exit the plane, making it halfway down the steps when Jesse wails, "No! Oh, my God! Uncle Reed! No!"

Swallowing hard, he keeps going. Everett is up head, limping toward the stairs. The woman named Teresa has her arm around his waist.

"Where's the map?"

"Right here. Everett holds it up. "I have not had a chance to look at it in the light, yet, to figure out the best—"

"Pardon me for interrupting, but I think I can help with the decision as to where to go."

Dirk studies the woman's dirty face. She is trying her best to seem helpful, but he senses a dark edginess behind the façade of frightened woman. "Teresa, correct?"

"Yes. We need to go to a place that doesn't have a nuclear plant, and where I'm from, there isn't one."

"El Salvador, right?"

The look of shock is fleeting, but it is there for a brief second in Teresa's dark eyes.

"Yes. How did you know?"

"Recognized the accent. I've been there before."

"I've only been in the states for a few years. My family has an estate outside of San Salvador. Like I told the others earlier, it's a big place. Lots of room for us all, and plenty of land to grow food on. A big wall surrounding it. We'd be safe there."

A rumble inside his gut is a warning: The woman is hiding something. "Have you had any contact with your family, Miss?"

"Sanchez. Teresa Sanchez. Sadly, no. But I guarantee you, we'll be safe there. No fear of radiation."

"I'll assist Dr. Berning to his seat. Why don't you help the others load the supplies? I'll make sure to talk to the pilot and tell him of your plan. Okay?"

"Of course. Anything I can do to help."

He waits until she is out of earshot while Everett up the steps and into the cabin. "What do you think, Doc?"

"Well, I believe she's correct about El Salvador, though I'll need to consult the map to be positive. If she's right, that's one hurdle jumped. A safe location for us to live, together, is another positive, if she's telling the truth. The downside is we won't be anywhere near a lab."

"True on all accounts."

Everett hears Jane's and Jesse's sobs. "What's going on?"

Dirk glances to the back of the cabin. Jesse is sobbing into Turner's chest; Jane has buried her face in Martha's shoulder. "Reed and Walter didn't make it back. They died while out searching for supplies."

"Oh, no. Poor things. Help me back there, please? I want to pay my respects."

"Of course, but let me ask you—do you get the sense Teresa's playing us or is it just me?"

"A little, yes. She's a bit too eager. Then again, if she's from there, it's not a surprise. She's probably worried about her family. I'm exhausted, and honestly, I don't care where we go. The only caveat is no nuclear reactors. I'll let you and the rest of the group figure out where we settle."

Dirk heads back outside. A flurry of activity greets him.

Kevin crosses the floor, sweat dripping off his forehead. "Got all the supplies loaded. Denaryl said the tanks are full, thank God. Hope the gas ain't been sitting too long."

"Good. Get everyone inside, and let's figure out exactly where to go. Teresa suggested El Salvador, but I've got my doubts."

"Why? It's what, maybe fifteen hundred miles from here? Denaryl can fly that distance standing on his head. I assume that's where the little hot tamale's from?"

"Yep, and she made sure to mention the fact there aren't any reactors near, and that her family owns a big mansion for us to live in. All safe and snug."

Kevin laughs. "And you aren't buying it."

"Not even with someone else's money. The only thing she can offer us is an extra set of hands. Did she seem strong when helping you load?"

"Not a clue. Haven't seen her. And I disagree. There's at least one other thing I can think of she'd be useful for."

"Shit!" Dirk spins around, searching for Teresa. The rumble inside his gut ignites into a flame.

Running at full speed, he races across the concrete. Sensing something is wrong, Drake and the others follow. By the time he bursts inside and notices the cockpit door is closed, his imagined fears become a reality.

"Open that fucking door, Teresa. Right now!"

"Dirk? She's got the drop on me. Back away and for God sakes, don't try to storm inside here or I'll be missing a body part I don't want to lose."

"What's going on?" Kyle asks from the bottom of the stairs.

Dirk's entire body trembles with rage. He wants to kick the door down and blow the bitch's head off. This is the second time in less than twelve hours he's been duped by females. Turning, he faces the terrified stares of the other passengers. "Looks like we're heading to El Salvador, people. Buckle up."

No one speaks, each appearing to realize their choices are nil.

Kevin comes up behind him. "Do we just stand here holding our nuts while she hijacks the plane?"

"As much as I hate to say it, yes. We can't risk a takedown. If she kills Dee, we're screwed. None of us can fly this thing."

"When we land, she's toast."

"I'm right there with you, Kevin. But, if she's telling the truth about a safe place for us all, then we're at her mercy. Only she knows the way."

"Bitch!"

"Oh, she's way beyond that. The minute we step foot in a safe zone, I'm going to slit her throat. She's more than a liability—she's a death sentence to us all—if we let her live."

ABOUT THE AUTHOR

Award-winning and International bestselling author Ashley Fontainne's works are available in ebook, print, and audio. Visit www.ashleyfontainne.net for more information.